DR✓

Circle
of
Strangers

Circle
of
Strangers

MINKA
KENT

THOMAS & MERCER

Published by Thomas & Mercer, Seattle

www.apub.com

Amazon, the Amazon logo, and Thomas & Mercer are trademarks of Amazon.com, Inc., or its affiliates.

EU product safety contact:
Amazon Media EU S. à r.l.
38, avenue John F. Kennedy, L-1855 Luxembourg
amazonpublishing-gpsr@amazon.com

ISBN-13: 9781662527012 (paperback)
ISBN-13: 9781662527029 (digital)

Cover design by Ploy Siripant
Cover image: © Irina Bg, © nizas / Shutterstock; © Jonathan Knowles / Getty

Printed in the United States of America

For M—I'm grateful we're not strangers anymore

PROLOGUE

PRESENT DAY

I wipe my hands against my linen apron and inspect my ruddy palms as the oven timer chimes. The clock reads 5:45 PM, proof that the last two hours have been a dreamlike blur.

"Georgie, Jackson," I call into the next room. I reach for my phone and close out of my cooking app. I've made this meal a dozen times and know the recipe by heart, except today. My mind has been . . . preoccupied. "Dinner's ready."

There's a break in my voice as I realize these are somehow the first words I've spoken in the last two hours, since I discovered the body in my garage.

The soft trounces of little socked feet against tile pull me from my moment, and I paint a motherly smile across my face while plating their dinners and pouring milks and conducting myself as if there currently isn't a fresh corpse twenty feet away on the other side of the wall.

The life drained out of those bulging eyes is an image I couldn't forget if I tried.

I don't know who did it, when—or why.

But I intend to find out.

"It smells funny." Jackson picks at his balsamic-glazed chicken. I'll admit it's on the dry side, but there's no odor.

My heart stops. Dead bodies don't turn malodorous that quickly, do they?

I compose myself. "You've eaten this plenty of times. I made it the same as I always do. I promise you'll love it."

He pokes at his garlic-parmesan risotto next. The contemplative look on his serious little face tells me he's two seconds from asking me to make chicken nuggets, but to my surprise, he thinks better of it and takes a bite.

Beside him, Georgie cleans her plate and polishes off her milk in record time. Since we moved to this quiet gated neighborhood in a cozy Phoenix suburb a couple of months ago, she's hit a growth spurt. I wouldn't be surprised if she's grown three inches already. Every time I look at her, it's as if her cherubic face has suddenly lost a little more roundness, a little more innocence. I can only hope that everything that transpired in San Diego doesn't leave any lasting marks on her. She isn't old enough to comprehend what happened, nor do Will and I ever intend to tell her, but losing her relationship with her beloved Nana has to be taking its toll.

"May I be excused?" Georgie asks, blinking up at me with her wide eyes framed in silky dark lashes. For a moment, I see my daughter as a teenager and then a woman. If I could stop time, I'd do it in a heartbeat. This world is full of horrible people who do horrible things—though as of two hours ago, there's one less of them.

"Yes, you may. Please take your dishes to the sink. I'll be up to run your bathwater soon," I tell her.

While scooting her chair out, she pauses. "But I wanted to ride my bike."

Her bike is in the garage—along with the body.

"Not tonight, my love." I inject as much compassion in my voice as I can in an attempt to quell the storm brewing in her eyes. Ever since moving here—to a home with a gated driveway in a gated community, I've loosened my reins ever so slightly in the form of allowing her to ride her bike in the driveway in the evenings.

Baby steps.

"Why not?" she asks.

"We're going to bed early tonight." I slice a chunk of chicken and drive the tines of my fork into its flesh. It slides in, and my mind

2

wanders to the purple-red stab wounds all over the body. There had to have been at least a dozen, if not more.

Whoever killed them wanted them deader than dead.

"But, Mommy," my daughter protests. "Why do we have to go to bed early?"

Will gets home from teaching his night class in three hours and I have a crime scene to clean up, but I can't tell her that.

"We have an early morning tomorrow. Your father and I are taking you somewhere fun. It's a surprise." I'm not sure what we're doing yet, but I've got to get us out of the house for the day. I need a breather, distance from what transpired, and a side of normalcy. Clearing my throat, I sit straight and fix my attention to my son. "Jackson, how's your risotto?"

His mouth full, Jackson gives me a thumbs-up and an energetic nod.

With heavy stomps, Georgiana takes her plate to the sink, then trudges down the hall to her room. Slamming the door in protest. Ordinarily I wouldn't let this slide, but tonight I've got more pressing things to deal with than a kindergarten tantrum.

Glancing toward the garage entry, I let my gaze linger a little longer than usual on the dead bolt in its locked position. My mind needs extra reassurance that everything is exactly as I left it.

I'd have called the police, but with the murder having taken place in my home and my recent text exchange with the victim being quite heated, they're going to have questions.

Questions I can't answer . . . yet.

"Jackson, if you're finished, please take your plate to the kitchen. Go pick out some pajamas and a bedtime book." He doesn't question the fact that it's still light outside. Fortunately he's too young to grasp a broader concept of time like his sister does; he only knows the order of his routine. Since time is of the essence, I'm skipping his bath tonight. If I don't wash and detangle Georgie's hair, it'll be a rat's nest come tomorrow morning. If it weren't for that, I'd skip hers, too.

I imagine gracefully straddling the line between domestic normalcy and the dire situation in my garage isn't something the average person could do, but to me, it might as well be an ordinary Wednesday.

Yawning, Jackson questions nothing. I silently thank the chewable melatonin gummy I gave him half an hour ago. It's not something I do often, but I have to protect them from this, and that means ensuring they're out cold and won't accidentally walk into a scene that could traumatize them for life.

With the kids preoccupied for a moment, I box up leftovers for Will and make a mental list of all the things I'm going to need. Bleach and a tarp. Gloves—leather or latex. A mask. It would be much easier if I could simply google this.

Thirty minutes later, the children are out cold, tucked into their beds in neighboring bedrooms across the hall from the primary suite. I stand in their doorways, watching and listening as their breaths steady and their chests rise and fall. Closing their doors, I trek to the laundry room to grab a gallon of Clorox before heading to the garage. With a damp palm wrapped around the doorknob, I draw in a deep, slow breath and prepare myself for the work that lies ahead.

With enough effort and a bit of adrenaline coursing through me, I should have no problem doing what I need to do. My plan is to get the body onto a tarp, roll it into said tarp, then place it onto another tarp in the trunk of my car. I'm not sure what I'll do with it, but I've got a few ideas mentally marinating that I'll need to finalize as soon as possible. There'll be logistics to work around, but I'll figure it out.

I always do.

Squeezing my eyes tight, I draw in and release one last deep breath, flip the dead bolt, and meet my fate.

Except something's amiss.

There's no metallic tang of blood hitting me like a wall. No trace of early decay lingering in the air. No lifeless, human-shaped lump in the northwest corner of the third stall.

With my heart inching up my throat, I smack the light switch on the wall, missing it on the first attempt. The overhead light buzzes, casting a sterile glow over spotless concrete.

The butcher knife is gone.

The blood is gone.

And so is the body.

1

FIVE WEEKS EARLIER

Reaching my hand into the dark recesses of our mailbox, I exhale with relief when I retrieve nothing but an electric bill and a political mailer. Only Lucinda could turn such a monotonous task into something that fills me with a little ping of dread on a daily basis.

It's been several weeks since she sent that letter welcoming us to our new home, the one addressed to my birth name, Gabrielle. I've yet to figure out how she got our address—and so quickly. I could see Will's scheming mother, Jacqueline, playing a part. Being locked in a jail cell gives that woman entirely too much time to think, but I'd rather she do her thinking behind bars and not in a world where her cell phone and bottomless bank account gives her free rein to wreak havoc on perfectly happy families.

The kids are under the impression that Jacqueline fell ill and went to live in a retirement home.

They're too young to know the truth—that Jacqueline stole my therapy records, learned of my horrific childhood, and that I was living under an assumed name—and used it against me. Never mind that everything I did was to protect my family from a psychotic mother who'd not hesitate to harm us if she could.

My diabolical mother-in-law was singularly focused on removing me from the picture completely, going so far as to hire someone to fill my daughter's head with stories from my childhood, stage a kidnapping in an attempt to make me snap, and push for Will to have me committed to a psychiatric hospital.

In the end, it backfired—landing her in jail on attempted kidnapping charges.

If my mother-in-law *is* somehow behind these letters, I'm not sure how she obtained our new address in the first place. Will hasn't even shared it with his father or sister, and we're renting, so our name isn't attached to any public sales records or tax documents.

It also makes no sense that Jacqueline would risk the safety of her son and grandkids by giving up our location. The woman had a copy of my therapy file. She read all the notes. She knew exactly what kind of person Lucinda was and the kinds of things she's capable of. The psychological games. The emotional neglect. Feeding me raw-meat sandwiches. Pretending I was invisible. Attempting to sell my virginity. I grew up in a special kind of hell with the devil himself—or herself—for a mother.

"Hey, hi!" A voice much too chipper for a Monday morning calls out from the other side of my driveway gate. A moment later, a hand flies in the air, frantically waving, followed by a grinning brunette bouncing on her tiptoes. "You guys just moved in, right? I'm Sozi Hahn. I live in the two-story next door."

I paint a smile on my face, tuck my mail under my arm, and brace myself for some soul-sucking small talk as I make my way closer.

"Camille," I say, punching in the gate code. The door swings open and she steps through in head-to-toe white—yoga pants with a matching sports bra and sneakers the color of undriven snow, a bold choice for this desert landscape.

"I've been meaning to introduce myself. I've seen you all coming and going. You have two little ones, right?" she asks.

I bet in high school she volunteered to give tours to all the new kids. I immediately imagine her in show choir and serving as chair on the prom committee.

I nod, offering as little information as possible to this friendly stranger.

"And your husband? At least, I assume it's your husband. The tall man with dark hair," she adds, though I don't know where she's going with this.

"Yes, it's just the four of us here."

"Well, welcome to Saguaro Circle." She awkwardly splays her hand out as if she's showcasing the cul-de-sac behind her Vanna White style. Sozi's laugh is nervous, which might make her disarming to anyone else. "We're kind of like one big dysfunctional family. There's a little bit of drama but a lot of love. I like to think that's one of the many charms of living here."

My brows knit. Why would anyone consider any of that to be a perk?

"You ever see one of those perfect families?" She rests a hand on a cocked hip. "It's almost creepy. It's not natural. I've always felt like a little bit of discord is healthy. It means everyone's comfortable enough to speak up, to voice their feelings. It's not normal for everyone to be happy all the time, you know? Authenticity is such an underrated thing these days. Everyone's striving to live these manicured lives that aren't even real." Sozi releases a quick breath and offers an apologetic smile. "I'm sorry. All I wanted to do was introduce myself and here I am lecturing you."

She lifts a hand to her mouth, covering her pretty smile for half a second. A delivery man in a brown truck pulls out of the driveway on the other side of us, all but craning his neck to check her out, but she can't be bothered to notice. Sozi either has no idea how gorgeous she is or she's simply pretending not to know.

Either way . . . interesting.

"I used to teach media studies for one of the local colleges," she continues. "One of my favorite classes to teach was Social Media and Family Studies. I authored the curriculum myself actually."

With her chestnut waves, toned physique, bronzed complexion, and megawatt smile, Sozi gives off more of a Pilates teacher vibe than that of a college professor.

Once again, I'm intrigued.

"You stopped teaching a class you loved?" I ask.

"After Ezra came along, we decided I should stay at home." Her emphasis on *we* is subtle yet undeniably there. "At least until Ezra's in kindergarten. You can't get this time back, you know? Teaching will always be there."

"You don't have to explain your life choices to me," I say with a firm but gentle tone. "I'm not here to judge."

At least, I'm not here to judge the kinds of things most people would judge. I couldn't care less what kind of cars are parked in her garage, where she gets her hair done, how long it has been since her last manicure, if she passes out with a bottle of wine on her nightstand each night, or what golf club they belong to.

My judgmental nature is more of the discerning type—can I trust you? That's what I care about.

Everything else is meaningless in my world.

"That's refreshing." Relief colors her eyes. "I love that. I guess I'm just used to having to explain that to other women, especially the career-driven ones. And I should know. I used to be one. Put a lot of blood, sweat, and tears into earning my PhD. Now I make peanut butter and jelly sandwiches and watch *Bluey* for a living. But hey, at least I get to wear jeans on Fridays."

She's trying to be cutesy and relatable, but I've never found humor in dumbing down the role of a stay-at-home mom. And I'd hardly venture to say it makes someone less "driven," nor would I dare to say it doesn't qualify as a career—it's one of the most demanding, thankless jobs in existence.

"I'm sure you do much more than that." I offer a kind smile and eye my front door, an attempt to signal that this conversation is over.

"I was thinking before it gets too hot, we should do a little cul-de-sac barbecue," Sozi says, oblivious. "That way you can meet the family."

She places air quotes around the word "family," then rolls her eyes at herself. Her cheeks turn a warm shade of crimson, too, as if asking me to hang out makes her feel vulnerable. Perhaps she's afraid of rejection.

"They're going to speculate about you," she adds. "If you keep to yourself, I mean. The rumor mill here can be quite . . . voracious. Best to get ahead of it."

She's giving insta-friend vibes now. I can almost smell the loneliness wafting off her, mixed with the faint trace of some expensive perfume.

My polite smile breaks for a moment. "They can speculate all they want. I don't mind."

The whole reason we chose this neighborhood was because everything seemed buttoned up and a world away. Privacy stacked on top of privacy. Towering hedges, concrete fences, gated entrances, private drives, and meandering roads a person could get lost on if they don't know where they're going. The first time we toured this place, I didn't see a single soul outside. No barking dogs. No kids chasing basketballs into streets. No men loitering in their garages drinking beers.

It was perfect.

Sozi's eagerness fades quicker than an Arizona sunset. I don't mean to offend her, but she can't possibly expect me to jump at the chance to rub elbows with a bunch of gossiping, desperate-housewife types? I refused to partake in the whole neighborhood clique thing in San Diego. I'm sure as hell not doing it here.

Besides, I stay plenty busy with my own family.

Not looking to join another.

"I'm so sorry. I just remembered I have something in the oven that I need to check on. It was lovely meeting you." I offer an apologetic half smile and trek backward, up the driveway. Since she has yet to budge, I'll have to close the gate remotely once she's finally gone. "I'm sure I'll see you around again."

"Of course. Don't be a stranger, okay?" Sozi's shoulders fall, discouraged. Regardless, she manages to perk herself up before giving a wave and jogging to the sidewalk.

There's something about her that reminds me of a neighbor we had growing up—Lisa Grable. On the outside, she was an extreme extrovert. A people pleaser to the nth degree. There was something both happy and sad about her, a quality I noticed even as a child of seven. I'd never known someone who could smile so warmly but project an aura of desperation at the same time. Lucinda saw through it immediately and wasted no time using that woman's weaknesses to her advantage, parasite-ing onto Lisa until she milked all the free babysitting, clothes, connections, and meals the woman could give.

I'm halfway to the house when I hear some sort of commotion from the tan stucco ranch on the other side of mine. Something shatters. A woman screams a slew of profanities. A door slams hard enough to rattle windows.

At the end of the driveway, Sozi stops in her tracks.

We exchange looks.

Curiosity getting the better of me, I head back to Sozi, ready to fire off a line of questions. Only I'm interrupted when a blond woman with mascara running down her cheeks steps out onto her front steps, a skinny unlit cigarette positioned between trembling fingers. Most of the driveway gates on this street are solid but hers is slatted, allowing for anyone to see through it at any time.

Maybe they're the type of people who like for their world to be on display. Some people feed off attention, good or bad.

"Everything okay, Mara?" Sozi shouts over.

The blonde dabs her wet cheeks on the back of her hand, scratches her nose, then tucks the cigarette in the pocket of her jean shorts, behaving as if she had no idea she wasn't alone.

"Hope so," Mara shouts back before disappearing inside without further explanation.

"Told you," Sozi says with a haughty smirk. "We're just one big, happy, dysfunctional family."

"But is she okay?" I keep a close watch on her door, though I doubt she's going to show her face again anytime soon. If there's any kind of domestic violence going on next door, I'd like to know so I can at least shield my kids from any potential interactions with them.

Growing up under Lucinda's reign of terror, I've made it my life's mission as a mother to be the antithesis of . . . that. I don't trust most people to be who they say they are, and protecting my children from those types is paramount. Their little minds are ripe for manipulation by design.

"No," Sozi says. "But she will be. She always is. She's like a cat. Always lands on her feet. Interesting woman. Complex. Funny, too—when she's not dealing with stuff. Get a few drinks in her and she'll have you laughing until your stomach hurts."

I can't remember the last time I laughed at anything, let alone laughed so hard I physically ached. That's the thing about sociopathy—it robs you of the ability to feel a lot of things. Sometimes it's a blessing, sometimes it's a curse. But most of the time, it is what it is.

"Bet you'd love her," Sozi says with misplaced confidence. She doesn't know me. She couldn't possibly know whom I'd love—or that I'm incapable of feeling emotions like love. "I'm telling you, let me throw together a little cookout for the neighbors. It could be small. Low-key. Maybe this weekend? You guys have a couple hours to spare Friday night?"

She's not wasting any time with this.

A cookout full of strangers is the last thing I'd willingly do with my free time, but now I'm curious. Besides, if we're going to be sandwiched between Sozi and Mara for the foreseeable future, I probably should get to know them, even if it's on a superficial level. Plus, you never know when you might need a favor.

"Actually, yes." I perk up. "Now that I think about it, it just so happens we're free this Friday evening."

After everything I've been through lately, what's the worst that could happen?

2

Boredom isn't something I thought I'd ever complain about, but things have been too quiet since moving here. It's a good thing. But with the kids safely away at their private schools, Will pouring his days into his new career in medical academia, and no new Lucinda letters to deal with, it's just me all by my lonesome for nearly nine hours a day, every day.

By the time I'm caught up on housework and errand running, I'm still left with entirely too much time on my hands, which is how I stumbled into my latest "hobby," if one can call it that: catfishing married men on dating sites—something I'm particularly good at if I do say so myself.

Years ago, my therapist told me people with antisocial personality disorders—especially sociopathy—are highly skilled at reading, influencing, and manipulating others. Some use it to their own advantage, for their own personal gain. Others use it to help those who can't help themselves. She said if I could fall into the latter category, it would be a way to use my sociopathy as a sort of superpower.

I'd hardly call myself a superhero, but in the three weeks I've had the True Spark app on my phone, I've already caught one married man. His name was John, and while it was wise on his part not to share his last name early on, he not-so-wisely let it slip that he was an English teacher at a local private all-girls school. When he wasn't trying to steer the conversation down a dark and dirty aisle, he mentioned he was chaperoning the school play this coming Saturday. I enthusiastically told him I was a drama nerd back in the day and asked the name of the play, not expecting him to answer.

But the idiot did.

I suppose that's what happens when you're thinking with your *other* head.

It took me all of five seconds on Google to find the name of the school, which led me to their website, which then took me to their employee directory, which was sectioned off by department. Sure enough, there was a John Bailey who worked for the English department at Cedar Mountain Girls Academy. His work photo, which I assumed was more recent, showed him to be a bit chubbier than the images on his dating profile. Less hair, too. His profile pictures had to have been at least ten years old, but that was neither here nor there because the point was never to meet.

With his identity in hand, I abandoned our conversation and browsed every social media platform until I found his profile—which was linked to a wholesome-looking brunette who shared his last name and who happened to also be a teacher. Clicking through her public photos, I came across one posted within the past week—a professional family snapshot of John, his wife, and their two adorable little daughters.

I sent a screenshot of the image to John, demanding an explanation.

He was my first "catch" and I wasn't quite sure what to do with him. I was like a cat toying with a mouse whose demise was inevitable.

I was met with staunch denial at first as he tried to gaslight me into believing it wasn't him.

When that didn't work, he claimed he and his wife had an open relationship.

After I asked if his wife would be willing to corroborate that, he began to panic—which included vague threats of blackmail—until I informed him that all of the images I'd sent him during our two days of chatting were AI-generated. He didn't need to know that I painstakingly edited those images, adding texture and tweaking the exposure so they wouldn't seem so perfect. Those images could've fooled anyone. Not to mention, he didn't have anything to blackmail me with. I never used my name nor was I moronic enough to move off the app and give him my phone number.

Chess, not checkers.

Lucinda taught me that.

She also taught me that certain men who are desperate for sex will say and do just about anything if they think they'll get it. John, unfortunately, was so desperate he was willing to risk losing his beautiful family for a chance to temporarily feel like a desired man again and not a bloated body in a stale, nonfunctioning marriage.

I get it. We all want to feel alive. But there are better ways to achieve that feeling; ways that don't involve shitting all over the mother of your children.

It took me all of two hours to decide to print off the screenshots of our conversation and anonymously snail mail them to John's wife.

I've never considered myself to be a girl's girl before, never having the need for such a thing. But I'd be lying if I said it wasn't immensely satisfying to do a lovely-seeming woman a solid. She's raising two beautiful daughters, enriching young minds, and sleeping beside a man who spent multiple hours over chat, begging me to call him "daddy" and sending me links to lingerie and adult toys he fully believed he would get to use on me.

I'd want to know if I were sleeping next to that.

With John's situation under wraps, I move on to the next guy—a never-married silver fox by the name of Sam. Every other photo of him contains a teacup Yorkie. There's nothing skeevy about him and his chats so far are fairly mild and basic, if not yawn inducing. He doesn't seem horny or desperate (yet). Thirty minutes in, he sends me his IG handle that contains his last name. A cursory internet search reveals Sam is not, in fact, married.

I un-match him and move on. I'm not here to waste anyone's time nor my own.

Next is Josh.

Also unmarried.

Then Jarod.

Also unmarried.

I un-match them both.

"Hello, hello," Will's voice echoes from the garage entrance. I close out of the True Spark app as quickly as I can, darken my phone, and place it aside, trading it for the colorful Colleen Hoover paperback beside me.

"You're home early." I dog-ear a random page and rise to greet him with a kiss.

"There's a blood drive going on and half of my students were volunteering, so I cut everyone loose a little early." He wraps his hands around my waist and pulls me against him. His lips are soft on mine, and he leaves them there a little longer than normal. If I could feel guilt, I might second-guess my new hobby.

If Will ever caught wind of what I was doing, I'm not sure how I could explain it in a way that would appease him. This saint of a man was quick to forgive me after everything that transpired in San Diego, for hiding my past, for living under an alias, for lying about the true nature of my relationship with my mother . . . but he may not be so quick to forgive me this time.

My reasons for doing what I did before were noble. I was protecting our family, protecting us.

My True Spark hobby is . . . a different kind of noble, the kind of noble only another married woman could truly appreciate.

"I grabbed the mail. It's on the kitchen island. How do you feel about going out for dinner tonight?" His tone is laced with golden retriever energy. "Been craving sushi lately."

I hate sushi but Will and the kids love it, so I always suffer through it.

Like the good wife I am, I feign excitement with a grin that stretches ear to ear. "Sounds perfect."

He kisses my cheek, gives me a playful pat on the rear, and loosens his tie before shrugging out of his houndstooth jacket.

Will's really been getting into the whole professor thing, even though he's technically an adjunct. It'll be years before he'll earn tenure, if he decides to do a tenure track at all. For now, he seems content with his new career in academics. Daytime hours. A dedicated office. Dealing with more students than patients.

Since leaving his job as an anesthesiologist, there are no longer hospital administrators to deal with. No on-call hours. He's significantly less stressed. And we have much more time together as a family. It's been an adjustment having him home so much, but it's also been a reprieve. I imagine he feels the same.

Arizona, so far, has been a breath of fresh air.

Dry, hot air.

But fresh air nonetheless.

"Will," I call out, trotting to the bedroom where he's emptying the contents of his pockets onto the nightstand. "I can't believe I forgot to mention this earlier in the week, but the Hahns next door invited us to a little neighborhood cookout . . . and it's tonight."

While I'm secretly thrilled to get out of our sushi dinner plans, I prepare myself for his disappointment. The man rarely asks for anything.

"Oh." He lifts his brows as if this is a pleasant surprise to him. "That sounds nice actually. It's probably not a bad idea to get to know some people around here."

"Right? That's exactly what I was thinking," I say, matching his energy.

Will cracks a half smile before leaning in to steal another kiss. He's been overly affectionate lately, which I've been correlating to his less-demanding work schedule. That and in a strange way, being here feels like vacation so far, like we're a world away from reality. The sensation will fade once the newness wears off, but for now it's kind of nice.

After everything happened with Jacqueline, I expected to see a more vulnerable side of Will. His mother worshipped the ground he walked on for over three decades, then turned out to be a deplorable, manipulative, calculating excuse for a human being. And it all happened so quickly . . . Jacqueline going to jail, the no-contact order, the cross-state move.

Instead, Will's handling it almost too well.

That or he hasn't fully processed it yet.

I hesitate to bring it up because things have been going so great, though it's only a matter of time before we have to address the elephant in the room. While I'm capable of numbing myself to the hardest of life's emotions, Will isn't.

"Thought I'd pick up the kids for you today since I'm home early." Will checks his phone for a moment, pausing to read a text before slipping it into his pocket. "Should I stop by the store and grab something to take over?"

"That would be amazing. Maybe a nice bottle of cab sav?" I lift my brows and bite a smile as I mention his personal favorite wine. Part of being the perfect Mrs. Prescott is knowing everything he loves and pretending to love it, too. It's why our marriage has always been so wonderful.

There's no friction.

No tension.

Everyone's happy.

Everyone's getting exactly what they want.

"Consider it done." He gives me a spirited wink before strutting off, and it occurs to me that while Will has always been a generally pleasant man, I've never known him to be in a constant state of exuberance, conducting himself like a twentysomething, giddy-in-love schoolboy getting laid on the regular.

I rattle that ridiculous fictional notion from my mind.

Will would *never*.

But watching my husband calmly weave around the room, a near-smile on his agreeable expression, I can't help but picture a ticking time bomb.

3

After Will leaves the room, I'm sifting through the stack of mail he left on the counter when I come across a slender white envelope with no return address—exactly like the one we received shortly after we moved in.

My heart stutters but I waste no time ripping it open, where a folded card stock letter waits to greet me.

> My Gabrielle—
> Your birthday is coming up, and I can't help but think about the ones I've missed since you left. I can only hope that you're happy, healthy, and loved. It's all a mother could want for her child. Just know I'll be thinking about you on your special day.

There's no signed name at the bottom, but once again, the erratic, tangled penmanship is unmistakably Lucinda's, and only Lucinda would include the word "my" before my birth name—a direct insinuation that I belong to her, a not-so-subtle attempt for my psychotic birth mother to burrow under my skin.

I've spent the last thirteen years evading this woman. The fact that she found me . . . here . . . is as infuriating as it is a problem. At seventeen, after a lifetime of torture and abuse at her hands, I attempted to drown her. And she would've drowned had she not woken up in a gasping fit of rage, threatening to kill me if she ever saw me again.

I left that day, made a new life for myself with a new name and everything.

But deep down, I always knew it was only a matter of time before she'd find me.

Lucinda was never the type to go quietly into the night, to let anything go.

I read her words over and over, attempting to decipher the coded message—and there is one. There always is with this woman. Nothing is to be taken at face value. Nothing she says is to be trusted. Everything is a game, psychological and deeper than the deepest parts of the ocean.

She isn't wishing me a happy birthday.

She's reminding me of the time she threw me a birthday party—my first one ever—then forced me to give away each and every present I received for no rhyme or reason. I cried, begged, and pleaded, and all she did was toss the toys into a black garbage bag and drop them off at some bright green donation bin behind First Presbyterian Church.

I begin to tear the letter before something compels me to stop. Carrying it to the office, I tuck it away in a desk drawer, next to the first one. I'm not sure what I'll do with them just yet, but I imagine this won't be the last of them.

I spend the rest of my day focusing on monotonous household tasks, anything but Lucinda's letter. She'd love nothing more than for me to be sick with anxiety over whatever she's trying to pull. For that reason and that reason alone, I refuse to give that literal psychopath another thought.

4

"I should check on Ezra," Sozi says before popping up from her poolside lounger Friday evening. "I'm sure he's still sleeping. Be right back."

He was supposed to play with the kids tonight, but apparently he isn't feeling well. Sozi wasn't lying when she said she'd keep it small and low-key. Other than Sozi and Austin and Mara and her husband, Oscar, there are only two other couples here from the neighborhood and none of them brought children.

Still, Jackson and Georgiana seem entertained enough by the sheer novelty of swimming in a pool that isn't ours.

The smell of sizzling burgers and grilled onions mingles with the sweet tang of sunscreen and pool chlorine.

Around me, laughter rises and falls, punctuated by the occasional splash and squeal of my children leaping into the deep end of the Hahns' pool. From my spot near the firepit, I take in the scene: Will, over by the grill with Austin, nodding along as he pretends to care about Austin's latest golf game. Mara, seated on a lounger nearby, dangling her feet in the water, tossing back her blond hair every time she catches anyone's eye. Her husband, Oscar, dark and brooding, nursing a bottle of Stella Artois, appearing lost in thought.

Mara and Oscar make a very attractive couple and seem fine tonight, but the events of the other day have been plaguing my thoughts all evening. The mental image of Mara holding an unlit cigarette, mascara tracks down her cheeks, is a stark juxtaposition against the

Minka Kent

current version of her—magnetic smile, cropped white denim shorts, a teal bikini top, and deep blue eyes practically lit from within.

Sozi swoops in beside me when she returns, a drink in hand and a mischievous grin lighting up her sun-bronzed face. Her strappy canary-yellow sundress shows off every line of her toned body and on anyone else might seem casual chic, but on her it screams desperate for attention.

"Having fun so far?" she asks, nudging me with her shoulder as if we're schoolgirls gossiping behind the bleachers.

Two more hours before we can use the excuse of putting the kids to bed so we can bounce. The night is young, but already I've had about as much painful small talk as I can handle for one evening.

"I am," I tell her.

Sozi rolls her eyes playfully. "Liar. You'd rather be anywhere else right now, admit it. I can tell. You can be honest. It won't hurt my feelings. Not everyone's a social butterfly."

She raises her drink and takes a slow sip, watching Will from across the yard.

"Looks like Mara's found herself a new hobby." Sozi arches a brow. "Better keep an eye on that one. It's probably best you learn this now, but she has a type."

My gaze flicks to Mara, who's at some point left her poolside perch and made her way to the grill. She's leaning forward, laughing at something Will said. The high-pitched sound of her amusement mixing with Sozi's warning is grating. Mara places a hand on Will's arm, only for a second, but long enough to make me want to storm over and swat it away.

I've never been the jealous type, but this isn't about jealousy.

It's about respect.

She has no idea what we've been through or what I'm capable of. Flirting with my husband so blatantly and unapologetically is a slap in the face, an insult to my intelligence.

It's obnoxious. All of it.

22

"And what type might that be?" I ask, my tone as smooth as the top-shelf whiskey Austin served us earlier.

"Married men," she says, her voice low, conspiratorial and matter-of-fact all at the same time. "She's been through two husbands already. Both left their wives for her."

My attention zeroes in on Will, who's completely oblivious to Mara's shameless flirtation. Or maybe he isn't. I've seen that look in his eye before—somewhere between hidden charm and amusement, fighting a half smile curling his lips. I can't blame him for being a red-blooded man, but this is just embarrassing—for both of us.

Taking a deep breath, I steady the storm of thoughts twisting around in my head.

I know Will inside and out, better than anyone else possibly could. He's been chipper lately, but that's only because things are going exceptionally well for us after a stressful couple of months. He's only smiling because that's what he does now. He's happy and he smiles. Constantly. It's as simple of an explanation as that.

Still, Sozi's words linger in the nighttime desert air, and a whisper of doubt trails down my spine.

"She's pretty," I say, because it's true and it's much nicer than what I really want to say. That and I don't trust Sozi not to repeat things. If she's going to gossip about me, the last thing I want is to come across as petty or insecure.

"Pretty dangerous," Sozi replies, nudging her shoulder against mine like we're girlfriends who've known one another much longer than a week. "I have a feeling you're too smart for her games, though."

Lucinda would eat Sozi for the sheer sport of it.

I could, too, if I wanted to—but I won't.

"Honestly, she's not Will's type." Before Will met me, he'd only had two somewhat serious girlfriends. I stumbled across their photos at his parents' house once. Strangely they didn't look too different from me.

She tilts her head, her dark eyes twinkling like she knows a secret I don't. "Oh, sweet girl, men don't have types. That's just a myth. All

23

I'm saying is she can be very persuasive when she wants something. Just be aware."

Sweet girl? She's being condescending *and* trying to pit me against a complete stranger.

I let it go—for now.

Across the yard, Austin lets out a distractingly loud laugh, clapping Will on the back. From here, the two of them look like they've known each other for years, not hours. It's uncanny, the ease with which my husband blends in here. Almost like we've always been a part of this cul-de-sac club and not the new kids on the block. I, however, still feel like an outsider. While it isn't something that bothers me in the least, I should probably do a better job at fitting in and projecting normalcy.

"How was Ezra?" I change the subject. "Is he feeling better?"

Sozi's expression falters just a touch before she masks it with a bright smile.

"He'll be fine," she says, her voice a shade too casual. "Just a little bug. I'm sure he'll be back to his rambunctious self by tomorrow. You know how kids are."

"That I do."

"Yeah, he'll be fine," she says once more, brushing it off with a wave of her hand. "But he's miserable missing out on all this fun. He'd just love Georgiana and Jackson."

"I'm sure they'd feel the same about him, too," I say, though I have no idea if that's true. My kids tend to like about anyone close to their age—but Sozi hasn't even mentioned Ezra's age.

"So, how are you liking Arizona so far?" Sozi's question pulls me back. She's watching me intently, like she's genuinely curious about my answer, or maybe like she's searching for something beneath the surface of my reply. That or she simply wants validation that this is *the* place to live. People were like that when we moved to San Diego, too—they wanted me to gush about how great it was.

"It's been a nice change. Hotter than we're used to, but a fresh start is exactly what we needed."

Her lips bend into a smile that's both warm and knowing. "A fresh start can do wonders. New faces, new places, new beginnings. It's like shedding your old skin, don't you think?"

"Sounds like you're speaking from experience?"

Before Sozi has a chance to answer, Mara's laughter drifts over again, and I look up to spot her leaning toward Will again, fingers grazing the hem of her cutoff shorts. Will says something, and she throws her head back, the last of the day's sun catching the gold streaks in her hair as she does. Something about this scene stirs a familiar itch under my skin. It takes all the energy I have left to tamp it down to a more manageable level. For a mere moment, I grip my wineglass so hard, it could shatter in my hand.

I turn back to Sozi, who's watching me with a hint of amusement, like she's imagining the maelstrom of thoughts running through my head. She clearly enjoys stirring the pot, which might explain her desperation. No one wants to be friends with someone like that.

She leans closer, her voice low. "Mara may seem harmless, but she's a shark. And the key with sharks is when they start to circle, you have to know how to scare them off."

"I'm not worried," I say, because I refuse to be. "Will's not going anywhere."

After Will learned about my hidden past and my personality disorder, he easily could've taken an out and bailed on our marriage, but he chose not to. If anything, he doubled down on his commitment to me by professing his appreciation for my actions, staying by my side, and picking our family over his mother's inappropriate behavior.

I think back to earlier in the day, that little creeping doubt that plagued my thoughts all because Will seemed overly happy.

Of course he's happy.

We are happy.

Happier than ever.

"I thought you liked Mara," I say as our gazes drift toward the attention-grabbing blonde. "You were saying all kinds of nice things about her the other day."

"I told you," she says with a sniff. "One big, happy, dysfunctional family."

"Just because she's your neighbor doesn't mean you have to like her. Maybe you're taking this whole family analogy too seriously."

Hard truths are always fun to deliver to those with little self-awareness. It tends to go over their heads, much like everything else, so you can get away with saying just about anything.

Sozi laughs. "You stick around here long enough and you'll see how it is. There's a lot of love and a lot of hate in our little circle. But at the end of the day, we always have each other's backs. It is what it is."

I loathe that tired saying.

Across the patio, Mara catches my eye and gives me a cheerful wave, her grin wide and innocent. I raise my glass in return, mirroring her smile. But all I can think about is the way her hand lingered a little too long on Will's arm and the way Sozi whispered about it in my ear like she was doing me a favor.

I dare Mara to try to take Will from me. She won't succeed, but depending on how stupid she is, she might die trying.

5

"Oh. My. God." I clap a hand over my mouth and sit up in bed Sunday morning.

Will was up before the sun, all but ordering me to sleep in while he made the kids breakfast and took them on a bike ride around our little community. Warm in my covers and slowly waking for the day, I made the rookie mistake of reaching for my phone. It'd been a couple of days since I'd touched that dating app, and still half asleep, I gave it a tap.

Out of the five hundred and thirty-seven "likes" I've received since Friday, never did I anticipate one of them being someone I know . . . someone who lives next door.

Oscar.

Scrolling his profile, I swipe through the three pictures he has until I'm certain it's him. His bio is empty—a typical telltale sign that a man is looking for a hook up or he's less serious. Makes sense in his case since he's married. The only other identifying information is limited. He has a graduate degree. He works in business management. And he's a Taurus.

I screenshot everything, just in case. And then I "like" him back and send him a message immediately. With my AI photos, he'll never know it's me.

The icon next to his name is green, telling me he's online.

He replies within seconds.

Biting my lip, I set my phone down, unsure of how I want to handle this. Based on what I've seen and heard, I can't imagine being married to Mara is a walk in the park. But cheating and victim blaming is never okay. Then again, if Mara was openly flirting with my husband at the cookout Friday night, maybe she and Oscar have an agreement?

I begin to type a new message to him: Quick question. And don't be offended. I'm new to this app, and I've had the unfortunate luck of matching with married men lately. Please tell me you're single. Truly single.

He replies with a quick: I am 100% single.

Groaning, I contemplate my next response. I was hoping it'd be easier than this, that he'd clarify that he's in an open marriage or possibly even on the verge of separation.

He replies again: How about you? Are you 100% single? Because I really don't like to share. ☺

Anyone can say anything online. Clearly Oscar has no problem lying. But if his most recent comment has a shred of truth, I can't imagine how he must've felt when Mara was making her rounds the other night.

I respond: If I weren't single, I wouldn't be on this app.

Oscar replies almost instantly: You have no idea how happy it makes me to hear that. You're stunning. I'd be the luckiest man on earth to take you out.

I reply with: Not so fast. I'd like to get to know you a little better first . . .

He types back: Ask me anything. I'm an open book.

I ponder which of the millions of questions swarming my mind I want to start with first, except the moment I land on one, the front door opens and closes, followed by the familiar cacophony of my children arguing over something inconsequential.

Oscar will have to wait, which is fine—because I'm going to need time to strategize.

This one could get messy.

6

I find myself at Sozi's Monday afternoon—not because I want to be here, but because I need more insight on Oscar and Mara's situation.

Sozi hands me a glass of chilled rosé, the ice cubes clinking as they settle. We're lounging on her back patio while the kids are in school, feet propped up on the wicker ottoman, the desert heat tempered by the breeze whispering through her covered pergola. The early-afternoon sun casts a golden glow over the manicured rock garden—everything in this neighborhood feels so pristine, so controlled.

"Mara and Oscar," Sozi starts, leaning back in her chair, one leg crossed over the other. Her eyes twinkle like those of a woman who lives for gossip. I can't blame her, though. The day-to-day grind of a stay-at-home mom can be monotonous and severely lacking sufficient adult interactions. Not everyone is cut out for that. "God, they're such a mess, aren't they?"

I raise an eyebrow, sipping my wine, waiting for her to elaborate. Sozi doesn't need much prompting. All I have to do is sit here in silence, appear slightly curious, and she word vomits the rest.

"They're the classic 'can't live with them, can't live without them' couple." She swirls her pink liquid before taking a sip. "Always fighting, always making up. It's like our very own soap opera. Who needs reality TV when we have the Morenos?"

"That's one way to put it," I say, thinking of the occasional raised voices I've overheard drifting through their windows lately.

"You haven't been around them enough yet, but I've always noticed the way Mara's laughter always seems just a little too sharp, too forced when Oscar's around. And whenever they're together in public, it's like nothing's wrong—they're smiling, picture-perfect, arm in arm. Did I ever tell you how they ended up here?" Sozi's eyes glimmer as she bites her bottom lip, anxious to spill more tea. "Oscar left his last wife for Mara."

My glass makes it only halfway to my lips. "You mentioned she had a thing for married men."

"Right. Oscar's wife—well, let's just say she didn't take it well. Started stalking Mara, following her around town, even showed up at her work once. Total psycho."

I glance across the yard to the high walls that enclose the community. "Is that why they moved here?"

"Mm-hmm," Sozi hums. "They needed somewhere safe. A place the ex couldn't get to. Our neighborhood is like a prettier, more peaceful Fort Knox. Keeps everyone out, even the crazies."

I nod, not needing to fake the understanding in my eyes. I love it here for those exact same reasons. The tall gates, the security cameras, the guarded checkpoints. There's something comforting about knowing there's only one way in and one way out. It's the perfect place to keep people—certain people—out.

As Sozi rambles on, a thought flickers through my mind: maybe everyone here is hiding behind those gates, keeping something—or someone—out.

Maybe I'm not the only one.

Sozi interrupts my reverie with a sigh, sinking deeper into her chair. "It's funny, though. For all the drama, Mara and Oscar always end up having each other's backs. They fight like cats and dogs, but the second someone tries to come between them, it's like they snap back together. Weird, right?"

"They're both cheaters. Maybe they understand each other better than most."

Sozi laughs, soft and throaty. "Maybe that's it. It's not like either of them is blameless. Mara's had her fair share of indiscretions, and Oscar . . . well, we know how he got here."

I roll my eyes. The thought of grown adults behaving like teenagers when it comes to relationships is obnoxious. "Sounds exhausting."

"Oh, it is," Sozi agrees, her expression softening as she stares out at the horizon. After a dramatic pause, she leans in. "I mean, I get why Mara wants to stay here. Keeping things locked up tight, keeping the wrong ones out of your life. I . . . well, let's just say I have some family I like to keep at arm's length, too."

The air between us shifts.

"Actual family members, or are these former neighbors you once considered family?" I'm teasing. She doesn't smile. Bad joke, I suppose. Or perhaps she doesn't get it. Sozi doesn't come off as the brightest.

"Actual family members," she says. "I have a younger sister back in Boston, where I grew up. Complete hot mess. I used to loan her money all the time—until she stopped paying it back. And my mother—if you can call her that—can't trust her as far as you can throw her. If I let her in my house and turned my back for two seconds, I guarantee all my jewelry would mysteriously disappear."

I'd take a kleptomaniac mother over one who served raw hamburger sandwiches any day of the week.

"Some of us win the lottery when it comes to the family we're born into." I take the tiniest sip of wine. I didn't want to be rude when she offered, but showing up at school pickup with alcohol on my breath wouldn't be a good look for me. "And some of us aren't so lucky."

"That's one way to put it." Sozi's lips press together before she continues. "I had an . . . interesting childhood, I guess you could say. My father passed away when I was eleven. Drunk driving accident. He was driving." Sozi sighs, swirling her wineglass—a gesture that suggests the irony is lost on her. "My mother wasn't exactly around much. And when she was, she shouldn't have been. She'd disappear for days, come back with bruises or worse. Sometimes she'd forget to feed us, other times she'd forget we even existed. It's probably why my sister is so messed up."

There's a strange tug in my chest, and I imagine it's something akin to empathy, or at least what empathy might feel like were I able to feel such a thing.

I almost feel sorry for her.

No wonder she's desperate for attention and validation and connection, no wonder she refers to the people who live on Saguaro Circle as "family."

Sozi glances at me, and I can see a flicker of recognition in her eyes. "Please tell me you had a TV-sitcom mom. Tell me she was funny and cheesy and baked cookies and took you to the park."

I sniff, contemplating how I'm going to answer this. It's no one's business—but it also isn't often I meet someone who can remotely relate to what I went through. Without a decent therapist in my life anymore, it might be nice to have a sympathetic ear once in a while. Not that I need one. But there are days that keeping it all locked up inside is akin to letting Lucinda take up silent residence in a place she's never been welcomed.

"I like to think there was a parallel universe somewhere where she was exactly that kind of mom," I say, sparing details for now. "Unfortunately I think she would've really hit it off with yours. Birds of a feather."

She's studying me now, her expression a mix of sympathy and curiosity, but there's a hardness there, too. One that I know too well. The kind that comes from years of fighting your way through life alone.

"I guess that's why motherhood's been so healing for me," she says after a beat, her voice more introspective than before. "With Ezra . . . it's like, everything I didn't get as a kid, I get to give to him. It's this second chance, you know? A chance to do it right. Maybe this sounds crazy, but it's almost like I'm canceling out all the bad stuff that happened to me."

I stare at her, my mind buzzing with the strangeness of hearing words I could have spoken myself.

It's eerie.

"Same," I reply, surprising myself with how much I mean it. "Sometimes when I do something completely opposite of what my mother would've done, it's like giving her the middle finger and hugging my inner child at the same time."

Sozi gives me a small, knowing smile. "Yeah. God, that's a great way to put it. That's exactly what it's like. It's almost medicinal to get to protect them from everything we couldn't protect ourselves from."

This conversation—along with Sozi's self-awareness—is unexpectedly deep.

I glance across the patio, past the thick stone walls and the locked gates, imagining a world beyond them that's chaotic and out of control. A world full of danger. But in here, behind these gates, behind these walls, I get to control it. I get to make sure no one can get close enough to hurt my kids. To hurt me. To hurt Will.

"Exactly," I say, my voice firmer now. "It's all about keeping them safe."

Sozi looks at me, something like relief in her eyes, as if she's been waiting her whole life to meet someone who gets it—and she has no idea just how much I get it.

The timer on my phone dings, signaling it's time to pick up the kids. If I don't arrive at exactly 2:40 PM to Jackson's school, I'll get stuck at the end of the car lane, which will make me late for Georgie's pickup.

"I'd love to continue this conversation another time," I tell her. While I'm not champing at the bit to discuss Lucinda in any kind of detail, I'm curious about Sozi's experience. Her overly extroverted, oversharing, desperate-for-human-interaction-persona aside, I can't recall the last time *I* had an actual friend.

It might be nice.

Keyword: might.

And I could be good for her. I could take her under my wing, instill a bit of self-worth in her, maybe even some self-awareness.

I could be an anti-Lucinda.

Besides, catfishing married men on dating apps isn't as much fun as I thought it would be. Some days it's more of a chore. Sozi might be a nice project for me. It'd be a win-win for both of us.

As I walk home under the golden glow of the afternoon, my shadow long against the pavement, I can't help but ponder on this little circle of strangers, each of us with our own hidden worlds behind our locked gates, our own secrets we're desperately trying to keep out.

7

Under the glow of my bedside lamp, I scroll aimlessly through my phone. Will took Jackson and Georgie on another bike ride after dinner tonight, and now that the kids are bathed and in bed, he's enjoying a long, hot shower himself.

Tapping on the True Spark app, I pull up my messages. I still haven't decided what I'm going to do about Oscar, if I do anything at all. I haven't messaged him since yesterday morning, so I've technically ghosted him, but I can't help but feel like I'm the one being haunted.

I should delete the app and abandon the project altogether, except the fact that it's taking place in my own backyard coupled with the way his wife's eyes seem to wander to my husband . . . makes it more personal.

> **OSCAR:** Where'd you go, gorgeous? You just going to leave me all by my lonesome (and very single) self?

> **OSCAR:** Waiting . . .

> **OSCAR:** I think you should know, while I'm horrible at sharing, I'm also equally bad at giving up when I find something I want. You're drop dead gorgeous and I want you. What are you doing this Friday? There's a new Japanese restaurant in the valley I've been wanting to try.

OSCAR: Or if you prefer, we can go somewhere a little more private and get to know each other better . . .

I fire back with something to test him: Sorry. To be honest, this dating app stuff is a bit overwhelming. I can't keep up with all the matches. I'm intrigued by you, Oscar, but you're going to have to try harder to convince me why I should consider you. Tell me what you're looking for in someone, what kind of partner you are, what a relationship means to you.

OSCAR: Fair enough. And not surprised. Let me think . . . You should consider me because once I have my sights on you, no one else exists. I'm diehard loyal. I'm possessive but in a healthy way. I'm generous in every way imaginable—emotionally, financially, physically. I have a great job and make more than enough money to provide a comfortable lifestyle. I'm just looking for someone to enjoy life with. Someone playful, someone intelligent, someone who can be my counterpart. I take relationships seriously and expect the same.

Oscar's response is clearly full of shit, but given that our conversation has been superficial so far, I've got nothing to call him out on . . . yet. Nevertheless, I reply: Have you ever been married before?

OSCAR: Yes. You?

I respond: Yes. Why didn't your marriage work out?

OSCAR: You could say we brought out the worst in each other. That and we had very different

definitions of loyalty. What about you? Why didn't
yours work out?

Again, he's spewing lies, but I type out a quick: Mine loved his job
more than he loved me.

> **OSCAR:** I've always found those kind of men to be
> pathetic. A job won't love you back or keep your bed
> warm. Smart woman. You did the right thing ditching
> someone who doesn't deserve you.

"What're you looking at over there?" Will's voice sends a hard start
to my heart. I hadn't heard him get out of the shower. I gasp and drop
my phone. Fortunately it lands screen side down. "Whatever it is, must
be intense. You had a look."

With his damp dark hair, a towel secured around his hips, and a
mischievous smirk on his handsome face, I momentarily envision a
horrifying scenario in which the phone did not land screen side down
and I have to explain to Will why our next-door neighbor is asking me
out on a dating app.

"Sorry. Sozi sent me this article and I was reading it," I lie.

"Oh yeah? You two becoming fast friends?" His lips curl up at
one side. He's always wanted me to make friends, but I've never seen
the point. Most friendships are transactional by nature. They've never
served a point for me, though perhaps that'll change with Sozi. She fills
the bored spots of my day and keeps me abreast with the latest Moreno
gossip. That's got to count for something. "What's the article about?"

"Kids and social media, the effects on mental health, that sort of
thing. She used to teach media studies or something. It's fascinating."

He changes into clean boxers and tugs a pair of jersey-soft pajama
bottoms on before climbing in bed next to me. Pulling me close, he
nibbles my ear and says, "Tell me all about it. I want to hear everything."

Thinking fast, I switch gears. "I don't know, I'm not feeling like doing much talking now that you're here."

My words, while cheap, light his eyes and seem to make him forget all about the bogus article story. In the twenty minutes that follow, I do one of the many things Camille Prescott does best. When it's over and Will's out cold, I close out of the app and retire my phone for the night.

I need to be more careful.

8

"Hey there." A vaguely familiar voice beckons me as I get the mail Wednesday. Before I have a chance to flip through the flyers and mailers and ensure there's no trace of Lucinda, Mara's flagging me down from her mailbox next door. "Cami, is that right?"

"Hi." For someone who was making herself all too familiar with my husband last week, I'd think she'd at least have the decency to learn my name. "It's Camille."

She strides my way in her ecru cashmere robe, her hips swaying ever so with each effortless step. Her blond locks practically bounce off her shoulders, slow motion, like a walking Bumble and bumble billboard. Tucking a strand of hair behind one ear, she gifts me a sunshine-warm smile that might charm the average person, but I'm far from average.

"I feel bad, we didn't get to talk much at the barbecue the other night," she says before biting the side of her lip. "Sorry you got stuck with Sozi."

"Sozi's been very welcoming." I've no desire to get between these women and whatever their petty neighborhood family drama may be. Besides, it's the truth. Sozi has been a one-woman welcoming committee at every turn—and bonus points for the fact that she keeps her hands off my husband.

"Well, that's good." Her warm expression is a contrast against the insincerity in her voice. "I was just about to enjoy my morning coffee if you want to come over for a few? I promise I won't talk your ear off like some people around here . . ."

Her eyes point to Sozi's two-story.

I get the sense she wants to vent about Sozi or do some "damage control" since this neighborhood loves their gossip.

I think about Oscar, his last messages to me. He was demanding almost. Desperately persistent. Too eager. A stark contrast from his sullen persona at the party. People can pretend to be anything they want online, though.

Mara toys with the gold pendant on her neck, a letter *M* and a letter *O*, and as she does so, the pear-shaped diamond on her left ring finger sparkles in the sunlight.

"Sure. I could use some coffee," I say. It's not like I have anything more pressing to do. The kids are at school. Laundry's caught up. The house is immaculate. I could waste a few hours trying to find more married men to catfish on True Spark, but something tells me a conversation with Mara might give me some invaluable insight.

That and I want to make it crystal clear that Will is off-limits.

9

"Come on in," Mara says with an effortless smile that implies we've been friends for years.

I step inside, where the scent of freshly brewed coffee lingers in the air, mixing with something floral—like an overpriced boutique candle.

With each step down the airy, double-height foyer, her house unfolds like the pages of an interior design magazine. Minimalist. Cold. A long white couch that probably cost more than Will's car stretches across the living room, artfully draped with a cashmere throw. Abstract art fills the walls—massive canvases of black-and-white lines intersecting in ways that look accidental but definitely aren't. The kitchen gleams, all high-end stainless steel appliances and marble countertops, untouched by the mess of daily life.

No toys. No crayons. No sign that children have ever crossed the threshold.

"Your home is gorgeous," I say, running my hand along the back of a leather dining chair. "It's like an art gallery. I'm not convinced that anyone actually lives here."

Mara grins, handing me a black coffee in a glass cup that belongs in some upscale café.

"Oscar and I appreciate nice things," she says with a shrug, as if it's that simple. "It's not like we have anything else to blow our money on. No kids, no gambling addiction, we're not big into traveling . . ."

I can't help but compare it to our house, where the couch cushions are always lumpy from the kids' forts, and there's an ever-present trail of crumbs no vacuum can conquer. Our appliances hum with the quiet resignation of a decade of use. But in this house, everything gleams, as if untouched by human hands—or the chaos of love and family.

No sign of human life anywhere.

Coffees in hand, we settle into the living room, Mara curling up on the long sofa, tucking her legs beneath her in a way that suggests she's relaxed—but her tight shoulders say otherwise.

"How's Will?" she asks, stirring her own coffee, eyes glinting with what I can only describe as curiosity. I make a silent note that she didn't butcher his name like she did mine—not that his name is easy to butcher. "He was saying he was a hospitalist before you moved here? I can't recall his specialty."

"He's an anesthesiologist."

"Oh, that's right." Her eyes illuminate, as if it's the most fascinating thing she's ever heard, and immediately I'm convinced this is an act. "I knew it started with an *a*. So he's teaching now?"

"Yes." I'm not offering her an ounce of detail if I can avoid it.

"He seems nice." Her eyes grow distant for a second. "He spoke very highly of you at the party."

I lift a brow. "That's what you two were talking about?"

She nods. "Pretty much."

Her hand was on his arm and they were cracking up . . . about me? I'm not sold.

"He said something along the lines of you being amazing in the kitchen and how he's amazing at standing around looking useful," she says, toying with her pendant again, dragging the letters back and forth along its delicate chain.

That doesn't sound like anything Will would say. True, he loves my cooking, but standing around looking useful isn't a way I'd ever describe him because he doesn't just look useful, he *is* useful. He's a competent man. I wouldn't have married him otherwise.

I smile—a little too broadly, maybe. "Will's great. I'm lucky to have him and I try to remind him of that every day."

Mara exhales a dreamy sigh. "You two do seem like the perfect couple. I always see him outside riding bikes with your kids. And watching the two of you interact . . . there's so much love there. It's like this easy gentleness. The way he touches you. The way you look at him. I just want to bottle it up and drink it, I love it so much."

How much has she studied us?

Is she always watching?

And why such an interest?

Up until the other day, we were complete strangers.

"What's the secret to a happy marriage like yours?" Mara asks.

I don't mean to, but I bristle at the question. It's personal. Invasive.

And she might be doing research.

"Complete and utter transparency," I say without pause. "We tell each other everything, always, even when it's uncomfortable. I find that it's those moments that bring us closer than ever. Our bond has been tried and tested. At this point, I'd say it's unbreakable."

Mara's lips twitch into a faint smile, though there's something about it that makes my skin itch—like she's mentally placing herself in my shoes.

"You're lucky," she says, brushing a strand of hair off her shoulder. "Oscar and I . . . it hasn't been that easy for us."

I sip my coffee, watching her carefully. "Marriage can be a complicated dance."

It really isn't. Not if you're with the right person. But Mara's fishing for sympathy and I'm fishing for intel. This conversation, much like any marriage, needs to be mutually beneficial if it's going to work.

Her expression wavers, and then, as if a dam breaks, she drops her head into her hands and begins to cry.

Oh, God.

I'm officially convinced I have a sign on my forehead, a beacon signal broadcasting to women like her that they can sucker me into being their free therapist by offering me food or drink, much like one of the school volunteer moms did back in San Diego. Sozi did it with a glass of rosé by her pool. And now Mara . . .

I sit frozen, contemplating my reaction. Hers is not the loud, performative crying of someone seeking attention. This is the raw, hiccuping kind, the kind you don't show just anyone. Then again, she went outside to cry on her front steps the other day. Perhaps *that* was a cry for help? If so, there are people far better equipped for her needs than me.

I put my cup down and inch closer, offering what I hope is a comforting presence but not too comforting—Mara needs firm boundaries and quite frankly, I owe her nothing after the way she flirted with Will last Friday.

"Oscar's been having affairs," she says between sobs, wiping at her face with the sleeve of her robe. "I just know it. All the signs are there. He's been working out more. Coming home later. Acting distant and withdrawn." She shakes her head, her laugh brittle. "I know it sounds cliché, but it's like a textbook midlife crisis."

Mara sniffles, her hands still shaking as she reaches for a tissue from the box on the coffee table.

"Oscar left his first wife for me," she says, drying tears I'm not convinced are actually there.

"Really?" I ask, though Sozi already gave me the full scoop. I want to hear it from Mara's lips. I want to hear how she frames her own betrayal.

She nods, biting her lip.

"I'm not proud of it. I never thought I'd be a home-wrecker. I never wanted to hurt anyone, but . . . he was so persistent and before I realized it, I was addicted to him. We all know addicts aren't known for making good decisions." She trails off, her voice breaking. "I guess this is my karma. I deserve this."

I watch her closely. "He's clearly demonstrated a pattern with being unfaithful. Why stay?"

Her gaze snaps to mine, sharp as obsidian. My question offends her.

"Because I love him," she says. "I know that sounds ridiculous, but when I'm with someone, I'm *with* them. I get these blinders on, and no one else exists for me."

Her words hang in the air between us, heavy with subtext. All I can think about are Sozi's words and how Mara abandoned Oscar at the barbecue to flirt with Will and Austin.

We clearly have different definitions of loyalty—just like Oscar said.

I take another sip of my coffee, letting the silence stretch.

Not unlike Sozi, the less I talk, the more she will, and that's the way I want it.

"You must think I'm pathetic." Mara's voice is softer now.

"I'm not here to judge." I offer another bit of reassurance in hopes she'll feel comfortable opening up even more. The more I know about her, the better I'll be able to assess her true intentions.

As I'd hoped, my words soften her expression and her tears begin to subside.

"Thank you. That really means so much to me." Mara cocks her head and reaches over, placing her hand on mine. "Oscar is my world. He felt like a prize at first. Lately he feels like a challenge. But now I don't know who I'd be without him. I don't want to lose him, Camille."

She's a beautiful and vivacious woman. I imagine men throw themselves at her feet. It makes sense that she'd be drawn to the unavailable or harder-to-get ones. It's clear now that Mara suffers from low self-esteem—a trait that makes some people impulsive and reckless because they're constantly chasing a fleeting feeling and what they want sometimes changes by the day.

Mara sniffs, rolling her eyes. "Oscar's got these . . . tendencies. He wasn't allowed to express emotions growing up—nothing good, nothing bad. So it all comes out now. In weird ways."

I arch a brow. "Weird how?"

"He breaks things. Throws things when he's mad. He's never laid a hand on me, but . . . sometimes, emotional damage can be just as bad. And he controls *everything*—money, decisions, everything. I don't work. He doesn't want me to. Most days, I feel like a prisoner to this beautiful life."

She gives a sad little smile, gesturing vaguely at the perfect house around us.

First world problems . . .

I bite my tongue to keep from reminding her I could find millions of women willing to trade their problems for hers.

"But I also couldn't imagine leaving it," she adds. "This is my home. Oscar is my home. I might be a bird trapped in a cage, but it's a pretty beautiful cage, don't you think? Things could be a lot worse."

She's one of *those*—the ones who complain about their problems, then rationalize all the reasons why they'll never do anything about said problems. The kind who are only happy when they have something to be unhappy about.

For a moment, I feel a flicker of something like understanding. Maybe that's why she was so flirty with Will at the party—maybe she needed to feel alive, to feel free, even if only for a few stolen moments. But just as quickly as the thought comes, I dismiss it.

Even if I could sympathize with Mara, I wouldn't want to.

She made her bed, she's lying in it, and she seems more than willing to stay.

Her crocodile tears are wasted on me.

Besides, for all I know, this could be an elaborate act. A carefully crafted story to throw me off the scent, to distract me from what she's really after. Maybe she's trying to get me to lower my guard. Maybe she's using her marriage problems as a smoke screen.

I set my mug on the table, eager to wrap this up.

"You know," I say, meeting her gaze, "if he won't work on the marriage, you shouldn't have to stay trapped. And if he's been your sole supporter, you'll get spousal support and half of all assets. I'm sure you could find a job. Sticking around with someone who doesn't value you seems . . ."

I let my voice trail into nothing. All the words I want to use to describe what she's doing are unkind.

I want to shake her. Tell her to find a little self-respect.

I also want to violently shake her and tell her to stop lusting after married men, but that'll have to be a conversation for another time.

She gives a small, humorless laugh. "It's not that easy. Even if I wanted to, he'd never let me leave unless it's in a wooden box. He's got quite a possessive streak."

Sliding her diamond ring off her finger, she hands it over, pointing to the inscription on the inside that spells out *you belong to me* in beautiful cursive.

It sends a chill down my spine, but I keep my face neutral.

"Anyway," she says, wiping her eyes with the back of her hand, "enough about me. I didn't mean to dump all this on you. God, I must be hormonal or something. I don't normally burst into tears like that. How embarrassing."

I find it difficult to believe she's embarrassed as she clearly has no shame.

I also find it difficult to believe she's some lovesick victim in her marriage.

I offer her a small smile but no words of comfort. There's nothing I can say that will sink into that thick, complicated, confused little skull of hers anyway.

As I leave the Morenos' perfect house, one so pristine it feels like it could be part of a movie set, I can't shake the suspicion that Mara was performing. This could've been part of her plan to infiltrate my happy marriage. In theory, if we became friends, she'd have more access to Will, more insight into my life and marriage, and if she were smart enough, she could position herself for the kill. It's exactly the kind of thing Lucinda would've done back in the day.

Then again, nothing about Mara screams intelligent. If anything, I almost sense she doesn't put a lot of thought into much of anything.

It's all surface-level emotions. Theatrics. Attention-seeking behavior. Nefarious people tend not to behave in such overt ways.

Maybe it's true that Oscar is dangerous.

Maybe he is controlling and broken.

Maybe she truly does love him.

Regardless, I refuse to let my guard down.

Not for a second.

10

I'm sifting through the mail after I return from Mara's when I find another slender white envelope with no return address.

Two in one week.

Holding my breath, I rip it open in haste.

> My Gabrielle—
> I hope you're receiving these letters. I've intentionally left off my return address. I suppose I'm afraid of what you'll say, hoping you'll hear me out first and give me a chance to show you how much I miss you. You were a precious gem of a daughter, and I often look back at our memories with bittersweet fondness. The other day I watched some neighborhood children playing hide-and-seek at the park, and it made me think of when we lived in that big white house on Birchwood where we'd play hide-and-seek together for hours. That place had an abundance of perfect hiding spots. I always knew your favorites and found you every time. Thinking of you . . .

Heat sears down my middle and I half crumple the letter in my fist. I didn't let her get to me the last time or the time before that. I shouldn't start now. But I'm beginning to get an idea of where she might be going with this little game of hers. It's some type of reverse psychology mind-fuckery.

We didn't play hide-and-seek.

When I was five years old, she asked if I wanted to play hide-and-seek. According to her, the rules were that you couldn't come out until you were found. There were times I'd be hiding for hours, waiting for her to find me. And there were other times she'd be hiding for hours— except I quickly learned she was never hiding. She was always gone, leaving me home alone, searching the old, drafty, expansive rental house for my "hiding" mother. When she'd get back, she'd laugh as she gaslit me into thinking she was there the whole time.

But even at that age, I knew better.

It was then that I learned real monsters do all of their hiding in plain sight.

11

The sheets are cool against my skin as I sink into bed that night, my head resting on Will's chest. The hum of the ceiling fan fills the room, soft and steady, and the scent of this morning's aftershave—cedar and pine—lingers faintly on his skin. I sit up and watch the shadow of the fan blades rotate slowly on the ceiling as Will readjusts his posture and reaches down to my feet, kneading them gently with his thumbs.

"How do you always know exactly what I need, when I need it? You spoil me," I murmur, letting my eyes flutter shut as he gently works a tense spot near my arch.

"You deserve to be spoiled," he says, his voice soft and affectionate. "You do so much for us."

I let out a small sigh, feeling the warmth of his touch melt the day's tension from my body. Moments like these make it easy to forget the thoughts that creep in when he's not looking. Right now, with his hands on me and his steady presence grounding me, it's hard to believe he could be anything other than mine.

Mara can make eyes at him all she wants. He's not going anywhere.

"You look so beautiful right now, all glowy and relaxed, eyes half open, like you're saving the last remains of your energy for me," he whispers, his fingers drifting from my foot to trace along my ankle. His voice is low, intimate. Toward the end of both of my pregnancies, when sleep was elusive, I used to have him read to me with that voice until I finally dozed off. It always worked like a charm.

I lean back against him, letting my head nestle into the crook of his arm. What we have looks a lot like love and functions the same. But what I wouldn't give to know how it feels every once in a while.

"I had coffee with Mara this morning," I say casually, testing the waters. "Saw her at the mailbox and she invited me in."

I've yet to mention the Lucinda letters, which have been taking up permanent residence in my thoughts like an old ghost refusing to leave an attic. I should say something, especially considering that Will knows the whole story. Except Will's been so happy since we moved here. I don't want to take that away from him. I don't want him to worry. Until I know Lucinda's endgame, I'm keeping all of this to myself.

"Oh?" He pauses his massage briefly before resuming its slow, comforting rhythm. "How'd that go?"

Will's questions never seem loaded, but sometimes I think he's better at fishing for information than I give him credit for.

"She got emotional." I draw out my words. "Apparently Oscar's cheating on her. She actually started crying. It was . . . awkward."

Will's hand stills for a second—so brief I might have missed it if I hadn't been waiting for it.

"Oscar?" he says, like the name tastes strange on his tongue. "*Oscar's* cheating on *Mara*? You're kidding."

Why he's acting as if this is shocking news is interesting—the two of them barely spent more than a handful of minutes together at the party the other night.

"Yep," I say, glancing up at him. "He's working out more, coming home late—she thinks it's pretty obvious."

Will hums thoughtfully, his thumb circling gently over my ankle. "Did she say who?"

"No." I keep my tone light, but I'm watching him carefully now. Will's always been a good listener, but tonight he's unusually full of questions.

He fires off another question. "Did she say how long it's been going on?"

"No, and I didn't want to ask. She seems a little . . . emotionally unstable."

He shifts beside me, propping himself up on one elbow. "What else did she say?"

I give him a lazy smile, hoping it looks as unbothered as I need it to. "Is it just me or are you oddly curious about this?"

He chuckles, brushing a strand of hair from my face before kissing the top of my head. "You're overthinking. I'm just making conversation with my gorgeous wife, and if that entails getting the scoop on the latest neighborhood gossip, so be it."

He winks and I force a soft laugh, letting my head sink back onto the pillow. But a quiet flicker of doubt sparks in my mind. If he is just "making conversation," he seems to be leaning in and absorbing every word of it more than ever.

I bite my tongue, choosing to play dumb. If he's fishing, I want to know what he's hoping to catch.

Will lobs yet another question. "Why doesn't she leave if he's being unfaithful?"

"She said she feels trapped." I add, as casually as I can manage, "Apparently he controls all the money and she doesn't work, so she doesn't think she can leave."

Will hums again, stroking his hand along my leg. "Sounds tough."

"She's not blameless," I say, my tone sharpening just slightly. "She admitted she helped Oscar cheat on his first wife. Kind of sounds like karma to me."

He blows a puff of air through his nose. "Since when have you believed in karma?"

I want to ask if I really need to mention the recent events that took place in San Diego, but I think better of it. We're having a lovely evening and I don't want to ruin it by mentioning Jacqueline. She no longer gets to exist in this exclusive little enclave of ours.

Will shifts beside me, his fingers brushing along my calf as he stares absently ahead.

Clearing my throat, I say, "Still . . . it's not easy, being married to someone with a temper."

I want to test him, to see how he reacts at the suggestion that Mara could be in physical danger.

"She told you that?" Worry lines spread across his forehead.

"No, she told me he likes to break things when he's mad." I pause.

Will sighs. "Has he ever hurt *her*?"

Something about the way he says it makes my stomach twist. There's a weight to his words, like they carry more meaning than he's letting on. I study his face in the dim light, searching for something—anything—that might give him away. But his expression is smooth, unreadable.

Will's an intelligent, observational man. He's got to be aware Mara was flirting with him at the party. And he's only human. I don't know many red-blooded middle-aged men who wouldn't get a kick out of some gorgeous blonde looking his way.

Plenty of happily married people have fantasies.

As long as he doesn't act on it, we'll be fine.

If he acts on it, he'll be throwing away all the hard work I've done to create this perfect little life of ours.

He'd be stupid to even consider it.

It doesn't get better than being married to me, and I don't say that out of arrogance. I know what I bring to the table: intention, intelligence, protectiveness. The perception of obedience and desire, a willingness to "serve." I make his life better in all the ways.

Mara could never.

"Oscar's the kind of guy I wouldn't set up with my worst enemy," he adds. "He's lucky to have someone like Mara, who stays by his side no matter what. Not everyone is that loyal—or tolerant."

I don't care for his tone or the fact that he's speaking about her as if he knows her on any level beyond surface.

"How do you know she's loyal?" I ask.

"I don't," he says, quickly. "Just assuming. If she's bothered by his infidelity, I'd think she's the faithful one in the marriage."

"We shouldn't be making any assumptions about these people. We don't even know them."

I roll onto my side, letting the silence stretch between us like a thread I'm hesitant to pull too hard on.

He brings my hand to his lips, depositing a kiss. "You're absolutely right. I was just trying to gossip but apparently I'm not very good at it."

"A for effort," I tease. "What do you think makes someone cheat anyway?"

I know the answer and it's as simple as it is complex, but I want to hear *his* answer.

Will gives a small shrug. "Could be anything. People get bored. They get lonely. They miss the feeling of being alive again. Or maybe some people just like to have secrets?"

His words hang in the air, heavy and loaded. I press my lips together, fighting the urge to ask what exactly he means by that. Instead, I let the silence do the heavy lifting, hoping he'll fill the space with something— anything—that might explain the strange unease curling in my chest.

But he doesn't.

He simply smiles, leans down, and presses a soft kiss to my temple.

"For the record, in case it needs to be stated, *you* have nothing to worry about," he whispers, as if that should be enough to make the doubts disappear. "You're it for me. It's you and me until my dying breath."

12

I pull into the driveway the next evening, my mind still half occupied with Georgiana's latest ballet class, the sea of high buns and pink leotards. The way she waved from the other side of the glass when she spotted me watching her from the waiting room, her face beaming with excitement. It's the small things like that—her innocence, her joy—that make everything I do worth it.

Lucinda would never—*could* never—be the kind of mother I am.

As I step out of my car and Georgiana dashes inside, I'm met with a trail of laughter coming from our backyard—low and easy, the kind that rolls between people who feel comfortable with each other. I pause, stepping quietly through the side gate and toward the edge of the patio, stopping behind an overgrown shrub to observe the scene in front of me.

Will is sitting at the outdoor table, a tumbler of whiskey in hand, his head tipped back in laughter. Across from him, Oscar looks remarkably different from the brooding man I met the other night— he's relaxed, animated even, his hand resting casually on Mara's knee. The two of them are practically sitting shoulder to shoulder, connected like Siamese twins.

And Mara is radiant, chuckling at something Oscar said, her gaze soft as she watches her husband with what seems like genuine affection. Oscar rubs slow, lazy circles on her knee, leaning in toward her as if they're suddenly a couple of newlyweds.

The whole scene feels . . . off. Like watching a play where the actors are reading someone else's lines. The Oscar from the other night was cold, distant—completely checked out. This Oscar looks attentive. In love, even. Not the kind of man who'd be blowing up the inboxes of random women on dating apps.

I stand there for a moment, watching them. Mara cocks her head, her golden hair catching the fading sunlight, and says something that visibly amuses my husband. The mere act sends a flicker of irritation through me, but I push it down.

Before I can make sense of what I'm seeing, Will notices me, his eyes lighting as he waves me over. "Camille, there you are. I saved you a seat."

I plaster on a smile, making my way over. Will stands and pulls out the chair next to him, as if this little gathering is the most natural thing in the world.

"Come sit," he says.

Next, he's pouring me a generous amount of pinot noir, the deep-hued liquid swirling in the glass. He hands it off with a sincere smile, his fingers gently grazing mine. Everything feels normal yet at the same time, it doesn't.

"Made sure you didn't have to cook tonight." He gestures toward the pizza boxes sitting on the counter through the sliding glass door. "Figured you deserved a night off."

Will's always been a stellar partner, but tonight he's going above and beyond. The only question: Why?

"Thanks," I say with a tight smile. "Where's Jackson?"

"He's inside. I just checked on him a few minutes ago," he tells me. "Little man's out cold."

Mara gives me a small wave, her smile just shy of too friendly. "Hope you don't mind us crashing your evening. Your husband is a very lovely host."

"Not at all," I lie between generous sips of wine. My eyes traverse between the three of them, trying to read the undercurrents of this strange little gathering.

Oscar leans against his seat back, his arm draped possessively over Mara's chair as he gazes at her with what I can only describe as endearing affection—completely at odds with his online persona and the image Mara painted.

While the lovebirds aren't looking, I shoot my husband a questioning glance. He clears his throat and straightens his posture.

"Oscar got home from work while I was outside playing with Jack," Will says, swirling his whiskey. "He mentioned some golf courses in the area. He knows all the best ones and wants to take me out sometime. Then we got to talking more and decided to have some drinks out back since the weather's so nice."

"Won't be long until we'll be frying eggs on the sidewalk," Mara interjects. "Everyone stays inside in the summer. Have to take advantage of these nicer months while we can."

Oscar is nose-deep on his phone. "I can get us a tee time at Tomahawk next Friday at noon if that works for you, Will?"

Will likes golf, but he doesn't love it enough to continue the conversation in the privacy of our backyard. Honestly, I can't recall the last time he golfed. It had to have been before Jackson was born. If he knew the thoughts going through my mind right now, he'd probably tell me I'm overthinking it.

But I'd rather overthink it than underthink it.

Will reaches for his phone, tapping on his calendar app. "I'm open. Let me put that in so I don't forget."

I told Will this man had a temper, that Mara cried over his infidelity and was afraid to leave him, and now they're here, drinking on my patio, and making plans like a couple of old friends.

Like the Morenos aren't completely unhinged and unstable.

After everything we've been through, why would Will invite *this* into our lives?

I wait until the Morenos eventually leave two never-ending hours later—Oscar with his arm wrapped protectively around Mara's waist— and only then do I turn to Will, setting my wineglass down on the table with just enough force to make a point. I've been so distracted, I haven't checked on the kids since I sat down. I blame Will for this.

"What the hell was that?" I ask, keeping my voice low but sharp. Over the course of our marriage, I can count the number of times I've taken this tone with him on one hand.

"Oscar got home, and we started talking. I was just being polite." Will shrugs, unbothered as we carry dishes and stemware inside. He leans against the kitchen island, casual, as if inviting a man I told him was abusive into our home is perfectly reasonable behavior.

"Polite?" I repeat, narrowing my eyes. "I told you he cheats on her. That he has a temper. And the very next day, you invite them into our house and feed them dinner?"

"I was hoping to get a better perspective," Will says, tilting his head slightly. His curious gaze is pointed at me, as if my reaction intrigues him more than anything. "You said not to make assumptions about these people, so I figured I should get to know them myself and form my own opinions. All couples fight, Camille. Maybe she was overselling it. They seemed happy to me."

I scoff. "Overselling it? You weren't there. She was a wreck. Practically dry heaving, she was crying so hard."

Will crosses his arms, watching me with that maddeningly calm expression of his—the one he wears when he thinks I'm overreacting. "Look, you know how people are. They say things when they're emotional. I just wanted to see for myself what their dynamic was like."

"Why?" I demand, frustration bubbling up in my chest. "Why do you care? What's your role in all of this?"

His gaze softens, and he steps toward me, brushing a hand down my arm. "Because you're home all day next to that. If things are bad between them, if you're spending any amount of time with her, I want to make sure you're safe."

Safe.

His words disarm me in a way I didn't anticipate.

Safety has always been my arena. He's the provider. I'm the protector. And we're both exceptionally good at what we do. This dynamic isn't something I'm used to.

Pulling me into his arms, he wraps me tight, breathes me in, and exhales slowly, his breath warm on the top of my head.

"You've gone to extraordinary lengths to keep our family safe over the years," he says. "You can relax a little now. We're on the same team. I've got us, too."

His words land in the space between us, gentle yet heavy at the same time.

"You know I can handle him," I say. "Oscar. If he ever tried to do something to me, the kids, or even Mara, I'd do what I needed to do."

Will cups my chin, tipping it up until our eyes meet. "I know you would. But you know I'd never let it come to that."

13

I stare at the screen, my fingers hovering over the keyboard, watching the gray bubble pop up and disappear as Oscar types and retypes his message the following morning. Finally, it lands:

> **OSCAR:** Apologies if I came on too strong—your photos and bio have me really excited. There aren't a lot of women like you on these apps. You're exactly the kind of partner I've been looking for, and I'd love to meet up and see if we have any sparks. I promise I'll contain myself. Believe it or not, I'm quite tactful (in public anyway). A total gentleman. Please consider it. I have a feeling we'd be perfect for each other.

Perfect. That word again. The kind of word men toss around when they think they've found something shiny and new to distract them from their dull lives. I sip my coffee, leaning back on the couch, letting his words marinate. It's almost amusing, knowing he's pouring his heart out to a collection of pixels—an AI-generated woman with flawless skin, glossy dark hair, and intoxicatingly innocent doe eyes. A mirage that only exists because I tweaked the lighting and added imperfections to make her feel just *real enough*.

He's desperate. So pathetic.

I respond: It's just that you seem too good to be true. I have a hard time believing you are what you say you are. How can I be sure you're not lying? Anyone can say anything on here.

The response feels like throwing a bone to a starving dog, and sure enough, the bubbles reappear instantly. Something about that line is like crack to sex-starved married men. It only makes them want me (or the fantasy of me) more.

> **OSCAR:** You've been burned and I get it. What if we just met for coffee? Something simple? You and me? We can talk and you can decide from there.

I roll my eyes. They always want "just coffee." As if that somehow makes them less pathetic or gives off nonthreatening vibes.

Another message pops up almost immediately.

> **OSCAR:** How about tomorrow morning? Kettlestone Café at 9 AM? What's your drink? I'll have it ready for you.

I type back: Fine. Black coffee. See you then.

I smirk at the screen. I have no intention of showing up. At least not inside. I'll cruise through the parking lot to see if his car is there, grab a photo for evidence, then I'll jet. I'm not sure what I'll do with said evidence. It's not like I need more proof that he's a lying, cheating scumbag, but perhaps the validation is all I need. To be honest, I'm growing bored with this anyway.

My phone buzzes with a text from Sozi, interrupting my thoughts.

SOZI: Need out of this house. Walk?

I hesitate for half a second, debating whether or not I want company, then type back.

ME: Sure. Meet you outside in ten.

I toss my phone aside and change into something comfortable—navy blue leggings, chunky New Balances, and a loose gray hoodie.

As I walk out the front door, the crisp morning air greets me. Sozi's already waiting by the curb, her hands shoved into the pockets of her light jacket. It's unusually tepid this morning. Agreeable by Chicago standards, but I imagine it feels like the middle of winter to the locals here.

"Thanks for getting me out of there," she says with a grin, falling into step beside me. "Austin's working from home today and he's driving me nuts. On the phone every five minutes while he's watching some financial documentary, which he feels the need to talk to me about for some reason, as if he doesn't know how much I loathe that stuff. It's mind-numbing. I needed an excuse to escape."

We stroll down the quiet streets of the neighborhood, the houses all bathed in a pale blanket of sunlight and blue skies.

It's silent here, peaceful.

Almost too peaceful.

"So," Sozi says, nudging me playfully. "What's on your mind? You've got that look."

I glance at her sideways, wondering if I should say it. I debate keeping it to myself for a moment, and I know damn well Sozi has a big mouth, but maybe that'll be my solution to this precarious situation. Sozi can let it slip that Oscar's on a dating app and Mara can find out that way. I can wash my hands clean of this whole morally gray thing.

With a little shrug, I let it spill. "I've been . . . catfishing married men."

Sozi's eyebrows shoot up. "You're kidding. Wait . . . what? How?"

"Dead serious." I smirk. "It started as a hobby, I guess. I find men on dating apps, chat with them just enough to discern their full name and if they're married . . . let's just say their wives end up with some enlightening information they can use any way they'd like."

Sozi exhales, her eyes wide. "Damn. That's intense."

Minka Kent

I laugh, a little more bitterly than I intended. "It's not as crazy as it sounds. It's just something to do, you know? It's like a game for me. It's fun to do some sleuthing, and I'm kind of pretty good at it."

Sozi chuckles. "How many have you caught so far?"

"Just one," I say. "Well, there's another one I've been talking to. I know he's married, but not because of any sleuthing I've done. It's someone I know."

Her brows wrinkle. "Someone from back home?"

"No. Someone from around here."

"It's not Austin, is it?" She slaps a hand over her chest, her expression falling.

"Nope. Not Austin."

She releases another breath. "Thank goodness. You'd tell me, right? I'd want to know."

"Of course."

"So," she says, angling her head in that way she does when she's prying. "Who's this current idiot? Would I know him?"

If Oscar's willing to be so blatant and careless with his indiscretions, I don't need to protect him.

"You have to swear you won't tell anyone I catfished him," I say.

She drags her index finger across her heart, drawing an X. "I swear on everything and everyone."

I pause for dramatic effect. "Oscar."

Sozi freezes mid-step, her eyes widening. "*Moreno?* Mara's Oscar?"

I nod.

The grin that spreads across her face is wicked. "Oh, this is too good."

"He has no idea it's me," I say, feeling the need to clarify. "He thinks I'm some perfect woman who gets him, but he's just projecting some fantasy. It's honestly concerning how fast he latched on. Very desperate. Troubled almost."

"Just be careful." Sozi winces. "Oscar's a piece of work."

64

I think about the shattered sounds coming from the Morenos' house the other week and Mara mentioning Oscar's "tendencies."

"He'll never know it's me," I say. "You're the *only* one who knows."

My words are a threat and a promise at the same time. I might as well be saying, *"I promise to confide in you as long as you keep my secrets. If you tell, I'll know."*

Sozi runs her fingers across her lips, pretending to zip them.

Message received.

We walk in silence for a moment, the sound of our sneakers tapping lightly against the pavement.

"You going to tell Mara?" She glances at me, squinting from behind her shiny Ray-Ban aviators.

"I haven't decided yet," I tell her. Half of me wants to expose Oscar's cheating ways. The other half of me isn't sure what to make of Mara yet, and I don't appreciate the way she looks at my husband.

I'm not threatened by her—Will would be an idiot to leave me for someone like her and he's a brilliant man.

"I actually had coffee with Mara the other morning. She told me she thinks Oscar's cheating, then she burst into tears. I thought you said *she* was the cheater?" I ask. "What's really going on there?"

Sozi's eyes flicker with something—a mix of amusement and exhaustion, like she's been sitting on too many secrets for too long. "Where do I even begin with those two?"

"Start anywhere."

Sozi laughs, a sharp, bitter sound. "Well, for one, they're toxic as hell. They've been cheating on each other for years. Mara can't stay faithful to save her life, and Oscar's . . . well, you know what he's like. Always looking for the next shiny thing to chase. He's got a new car in his driveway every six months. Every outfit he wears looks like it came straight off a high-end department store mannequin. Even his skin is flawless. People who are too perfectionistic, too in control, scare me."

"Yeah, but that doesn't make him toxic." I can't believe I'm defending Oscar.

"No, I know. I'm just painting a picture," she elaborates. "He comes off as this clean-cut, business-man type, but you can tell there's something deep below his surface. You can see it in his eyes, his body language. Something's repressed. Secrets. Emotions. Rage. I don't know."

I glance at her, waiting for more.

"And Mara," Sozi continues. "She's always been very reactive, impulsive. For better or worse. You put two people like that in the same room, let alone let them marry each other? And it's a recipe for disaster. The two of them have a lot of highs and lows, probably more lows than highs, but nothing much in between."

Makes sense given the lovey-dovey way they were behaving in my backyard last night.

Some couples are addicted to that roller-coaster ride.

"Thing is," Sozi adds, "they fight like hell, but they always come back to each other. It's almost impressive, in a sick way. She's never going to leave him, you know. Not really. And he won't let her go either."

She's confirming exactly what Mara told me, though I imagine Mara has told Sozi this as well. For someone who lives in a private community, Mara's not exactly a private person.

"Why not?" I ask, genuinely curious. "If he's looking for other women, he's not happy with her. He should let her go."

"Because they're addicted to the chaos. Oscar loves a challenge and Mara loves attention and validation, she loves to feel chosen."

Sozi confirms my theory that Mara suffers from low self-esteem.

"Here's the thing about Mara," Sozi goes on, lowering her voice conspiratorially. "She's a lot better at playing the victim than people realize. Don't get me wrong—Oscar's no saint. But Mara? She knows exactly how to twist things to make people feel sorry for her."

I file that away, remembering the tears Mara shed over coffee the other morning.

"And Oscar?" I ask. "What's his deal?"

Sozi shakes her head, her expression darkening.

"He's complicated. His temper's real, but it's more than that. He's the kind of guy who needs control. Everything has to be on his terms—when they fight, when they make up, everything. And if Mara ever tried to leave him for real?" She lets out a humorless laugh. "Let's just say it wouldn't be pretty."

We walk a little farther, the weight of this disturbing intel settling between us. With all the conviction in her voice and a distinct lack of details to back up her claims, I have to wonder what she's not telling me.

"Sounds like a mess," I say.

"Oh, it is," Sozi replies. "That's why I stay far away from their drama. Trust me, it's safer that way. I suggest you keep them at an arm's length, too."

"Will and Oscar are supposed to go golfing sometime."

Sozi rolls her eyes. "He's probably going to try to sell him some financial product from his firm. That's all that is. He's a financial adviser and he makes commission off that stuff. Your husband's a doctor. You have money. He's not looking to make a new friend, trust me."

"Good to know." If I told Will, he'd likely tell me he's perfectly capable of telling people no.

"So, what *are* you going to do with this Oscar thing?" Sozi asks, her tone light but curious.

"I haven't decided yet," I say, staring out onto a lifeless street. "He thinks he's meeting me for coffee tomorrow. Well, not me, but the woman he thinks he's talking to. If he shows, I'll have proof, but after that, I'm probably going to wash my hands of this. Sounds like the two of them deserve each other."

Sozi gives me an ornery smirk, shaking her head as we turn back toward our cul-de-sac. "Well, whatever happens, keep me in the loop, pretty please. I get just as bored here as you do some days."

14

I lean against the kitchen counter the next morning, coffee mug warm in my palms as I watch Will grab his keys from the hook by the door. He's already dressed for his Saturday class—crisp white shirt, navy blazer, dark jeans, and those tortoiseshell glasses I love. His contacts must be bothering him again, but I don't mind. The frames make him look more professor than doctor—a man who could spend hours debating medical studies or grading papers in a sunlit office. It's a good look for him.

Salt-and-pepper streaks at his temples catch the morning light. No denying the man looks gorgeous, and unfairly, he's only gotten better with age, like a rare bottle of wine. He runs a hand through his chocolate-brown hair, and I catch the faintest hint of something new—a scent that isn't quite familiar.

"New cologne?" I ask, tilting my head and inhaling the sharp smell of pepper and leather and vetiver. No hint of the familiar cedar aroma I've come to associate with him.

Will glances at me over his shoulder, a playful smile curving his lips. "Yeah. Been wearing the same stuff since the day we met. Wanted to try something different. You like it?"

His expression is eager, like he's silently inviting my praise and approval.

I inhale once more, softer this time, catching all the warm, woodsy notes. It's subtle, but it lingers, grounding him in a way that makes me want to pull him close.

"It suits you," I say, trying to keep my tone light despite the voice in the back of my head telling me that everything's changing—almost too fast.

Will's really taking this fresh start thing to heart.

"Glad to hear it." He presses a smiling kiss against my mouth before taking his attaché off the island. "If you hated it, I'd have to return it."

I lean against the counter, arms crossed, studying him like he's a puzzle with pieces that don't quite fit. He smells good, looks even better—but that flicker of doubt still stirs in the back of my mind.

"So, lunch today?" I ask, trying not to sound too eager. We'd planned to meet at a little bistro downtown—a rare chance to steal some time just for us.

Will winces, his mouth pulling into an apologetic frown. "About that . . . I won't be able to make it today. A couple of my students asked if we could meet during lunch. They're struggling with some assignments. How's Monday look for you? I'll be free around one."

The words are casual, perfectly reasonable, but they land wrong. My brain catalogs them like evidence in a case I never dreamed I'd be building. He's been too happy lately. Too eager to please. He's given himself a makeover. And now he's wearing a new scent.

It could all mean nothing.

Or not.

I press my lips together, nodding slowly. "I see."

Will notices the shift immediately. He sets his bag down, stepping toward me, concern flickering in his eyes. "Hey. Don't give me that frown. I'll make it up to you, okay? I promise."

I force a tight smile, though it feels more like a mask than a real expression.

"It's fine," I lie. It's not fine. He knew we had plans. He was the one who made them in the first place. He easily could've worked around those plans. I can't help but feel I'm no longer a top priority for him, and that's concerning. "I know you're busy."

He tilts his head, studying me like he can see right through me. And just as I'm about to pull away, he steps closer, wrapping his arms around me. I feel the weight of him—solid, familiar, grounding—and for a moment, I let myself sink into it.

"Camille," he murmurs, brushing his lips against my temple. "Thank you for everything you do for me . . . for the kids. I'd be lost without you. Truly."

His words soothe the sharp edges of my doubts. He kisses my forehead, lingering just long enough to make me believe he means it, like I'm the most important person in his world.

I close my eyes, inhaling the scent of his new cologne, letting his warmth settle deep in my bones. In this moment, with his arms around me and his breath brushing my skin, it's easy to believe that everything is exactly as it seems. That he's the same loving, loyal husband I married. That my doubts are just shadows—things without substance or merit.

When he pulls back, he presses one last kiss to my lips.

"I love you," he whispers, the words low and certain.

"I love you, too," I say, my voice barely audible.

Long before Will knew nothing about my antisocial personality disorder or the fact that I can't feel love the way he can, I always said the words back. They might be hollow for me, but they've always meant something to him. I imagine they still do despite knowing what he now knows. Perhaps they're more important than ever, especially since we established that love is a choice, an act of commitment, a decision. Not merely a feeling.

He gives me a half-cocked smile—one that always makes me feel like everything's going to be okay—and picks up his bag again.

"Can't wait to see you tonight," he says, opening the door. "Miss you already."

I stand, watching as he walks out into the morning light, his figure crisp and polished, every bit the handsome, capable man I've always known. He waves once before climbing into his Audi, and I wave back, the gesture automatic, like some robotic Stepford Wife with a pleasant expression on my face that hides the maelstrom of thoughts swirling inside me.

As he pulls away, the doubt tries to creep in again, but I shove it down, telling myself it's nothing.

It's just a meeting with students.

Just a new cologne.

He's just been in a good mood because we're happier here.

He's going above and beyond out of appreciation, not guilt.

None of it means he's cheating.

I remind myself that Will has always been there for me, always steady and true. But the scent of his cologne still lingers in the kitchen air, faint but persistent, like a whisper I can't ignore.

15

I park in the front row at Kettlestone Café five minutes before nine, my hair tucked into a baseball cap and oversized sunglasses covering my face. It takes all of three seconds for me to determine this disguise—if I can call it that—is ridiculous.

The windows of the café are tinted, making it impossible to see through them. I cruised through the parking lot before I got here to check for Oscar's Tesla, but apparently everyone in the greater Phoenix area who owns a Tesla decided to come here at the same time today.

Exhaling, I flip my visor, kill the engine, and head inside to grab a coffee.

The line is long—reaching the door. And the sickeningly sweet smell of pastries and burnt coffee floods my lungs. If Oscar wanted to impress his online date, he could've at least chosen a nicer place.

I move to the end of the line, counting at least twelve people ahead of me. This isn't going to be a quick in-and-out.

Scanning the room, there's no trace of Oscar anywhere. As desperate as he was to make this happen, I can't imagine he'd ghost me.

Dragging in a lungful of coffee-shop air, I pull out my phone and check the app. No new messages other than the one he sent last night telling me how excited he was to finally meet me.

The bells on the door chime behind me, and I darken the screen before anyone has a chance to see me checking a godforsaken dating app—except apparently I'm not fast enough.

"Camille?" A familiar gruff voice fills my ear.

I turn on my heels and I'm immediately met with Oscar's dark, cutting features.

The expression on his face is nothing short of unsettling. "Are you *fucking* serious?"

My stomach falls.

He saw.

16

"So. How was coffee?" Sozi asks with a sly grin on Monday, nudging me with her elbow. The crisp morning air clings to my skin as we power walk through the neighborhood, our sneakers tapping in sync along the quiet, manicured streets.

"I ended up not going," I lie.

It turns out Sozi and Mara weren't being dramatic when they said Oscar was troubled. After he saw my screen, I played dumb. I gaslit as best I could. But the man's eyes turned a deeper shade of dark. A storm was brewing inside him. All I could think about was the fact that he lives next to me and my family, that I'd never be able to explain this to Will in a way he'd understand, that moving the kids (yet again) would be awful for them now that they're settling in so well.

So I folded.

We sat down at a table in the corner and I apologized—even though I didn't mean it.

I swore my secrecy, played it off like I was some dumb, bored housewife.

I let him watch as I deleted each and every screenshot of our conversation, then deleted my dating profile and the app altogether.

I placated him as best as I could, faux tears and all. I promised him nothing would come of this, though nothing seemed satisfactory enough. His shoulders remained tense and the murderous look in his eyes remained.

I'd seen that look before, a lifetime ago, on my mother's face.

"If a word of this gets out, you understand it's not going to end well for you," he said under his breath, his car keys still clenched tight in his fist. He didn't elaborate. He didn't need to and besides, I didn't want him to. My imagination fills in these kinds of blanks just fine on its own.

It killed me to cower to that pathetic man, but my hands were tied.

Keeping my family together is worth more to me than the satisfaction of being right.

"I actually ended up canceling on him," I add. "Then I deleted the app completely. Honestly I want nothing to do with the Morenos anymore."

"You going to relay that to your husband? I saw him chatting with Mara last night," she says, her voice light but pointed.

My steps falter for a fraction of a second. He doesn't know anything about the dating app situation, but he's well aware of my feelings about the Morenos and inviting them into our world.

"When?" I ask.

She turns her head toward me, her wavy ponytail bouncing. "I saw them out at the end of the driveway, maybe around seven or so. Looked like they were having a pretty engaging conversation. Your son kept wanting Will to throw the Wiffle ball but Will seemed a little preoccupied."

My stomach tightens. He went outside to play catch with Jackson after dinner. That must've been when it happened.

I don't appreciate Sozi stirring the pot—but on the other hand, this is the kind of information I'd like to have, so I act appreciative.

"I'm glad you told me. I had no idea," I say.

Sozi scoffs, her lips curling into a knowing smirk. "Mara always seems to find an excuse to linger around other people's husbands."

"Has she ever lingered around Austin?"

She sniffs. "She knows better."

I arch a brow, wondering what that means. Sozi seems harmless. Then again, so do I.

My mind races as I stare at the walking trail ahead.

Why didn't Will mention this?

And what were they talking about?

"I just think it's interesting, Mara plays the victim to you and then she flirts with your husband. *Again.*" Sozi adds fuel to an already crackling fire. "It's obvious what she's trying to do. I'm kind of embarrassed for her, honestly. Takes a special kind of person to want to break up a happy home."

Flirting doesn't mean she's trying to break up a happy home.

But it's worth noting.

Especially since it's apparently becoming a thing now.

I glance at Sozi from the corner of my eye. She's easy to talk to, easy to walk with—our steps always matching, our conversations effortless. But beneath her sunny demeanor, I know there's a sharpness, a shrewdness that's always watching, always assessing. Her bubbly, college co-ed persona could easily be a mask she wears. It makes her disarming, likeable even.

I pull my hoodie tighter around me, the morning chill suddenly feeling sharper. Sozi might be right—Mara's flirtations, her tearful confessions, her innocent act—it all feels suspect.

"Keep your friends close," I say, more to myself than to Sozi, "and your enemies closer."

Sozi's eyes glint with approval. "You're catching on quick."

We walk in silence for a few minutes, the only sound the steady rhythm of our footsteps and the occasional hum of a luxury car passing by.

"Hey, do me a favor and don't mention anything I told you about Oscar to anyone," I say. "I shouldn't have gotten involved. It's not my place."

Sozi almost scoffs, as if my request is insulting. "I already gave you my word. Everything you tell me goes into a vault."

I'm not so sure I believe her, so I double down. "Okay. I trust you. You're the only one who knows. If this gets out—"

She places her hand on my arm, giving it a tight squeeze that leaves an ache the second she lets go. "Stop this. I promise, no one will ever know."

17

"Okay, so before Oscar," Mara begins, swirling the last bit of ice in her glass, "I was a hairstylist. Before that, I was a receptionist at my uncle's law firm."

The last thing I expected today was for Mara to invite herself over for drinks by the pool, but it's an unseasonably warm day and I've been haunted by Sozi's words since our walk earlier—*Mara plays the victim to you and then she flirts with your husband.*

I promised Oscar I wouldn't breathe a word to anyone, but giving his wife the cold shoulder out of nowhere would raise more suspicions than anything.

Being here is unfortunately necessary—for more reasons than one.

The early-afternoon sun glints off the cerulean pool, casting shimmering patterns across the water as Mara and I sit side by side in rattan lounge chairs, me sipping iced tea, her indulging in a 1:00 PM glass of rosé. The warmth is pleasant, but tension simmers beneath the surface—something unsaid, hovering between us.

Mara adjusts her oversized sunglasses and leans back, her body languid and relaxed as if she's completely at home here. I observe her from the corner of my eye.

I raise an eyebrow. "Really? A hairstylist? I could see that. Your hair always looks like you just left the salon."

She grins. "Yeah. I loved it. I was good at it, too."

"Is that how you met Oscar?"

Mara's smile widens.

"He was one of my clients. He came in the first time needing a cut for some big corporate event, but after that, it became a regular thing. Once a month at first. Then every two weeks." She pauses, glancing at me over her sunglasses. "And every time he came in . . . butterflies. And not just any kind. They were intense. Made my whole body warm. Made me lose my train of thought. Every time he was in my chair, it was like time stood still. I've been around my fair share of men and it was just different with him. I'm not usually into that woo-woo stuff, but I swear it felt like our souls were doing the talking and we were just there."

Her voice takes on a dreamy, nostalgic quality, as if she's talking about the love story of a lifetime and not that of a young, impressionable hairstylist and a handsome, persistent married man.

She sighs, a soft, wistful sound. "No one had ever made me feel that way before. I don't think anyone ever will again."

I take a slow sip of my drink, keeping my expression neutral. "He was married, though."

"Oh, I know," she says with a small laugh. "I asked him about his wife, you know, just making conversation like I did with all my clients. After a while, he told me he wasn't happy, that he was planning to leave her. This was before he'd even asked me on a date. It had been strictly professional up until then."

I raise an eyebrow. I'd love to believe her.

"The first time he asked me out, I said no," Mara continues. "And the second time. And the third. But Oscar is very . . . tenacious when he wants something."

Her words settle heavily in the space between us. *Tenacious.* I've seen that look in his eyes—just a flicker of it—when he's with her. A man who doesn't take no for an answer. A man who blows up the inbox of a dating app stranger he hardly knows, begging and then all but demanding a meetup.

A man who makes threats with nothing more than a handful of words and a remarkable kind of darkness in his eyes.

Mara sighs and adjusts the strap of her skimpy lavender bikini top.

"Eventually, I gave in. Maybe I shouldn't have, but . . ." She trails off, her eyes clouding with something I can't quite read. "He left his wife soon after. She didn't take it well. She blamed me, of course."

"How bad was it?" I ask, curious despite myself.

"Bad enough that we had to get a protective order. She'd follow me around, send me threats. It was scary."

I shift in my seat, feeling the heat of the sun—and her story—press against my skin.

"Do you ever wonder if he was lying to you about planning to leave his wife? Maybe he was telling you that so you'd go on a date with him?" I ask.

"I can see why you'd think that, but no," she says with the misplaced confidence of a lovestruck, naive woman. If only she could read the messages that were once on my phone, the ones where he reiterates how very single he currently is.

"Men say all kinds of things when they want you," I tell her.

"Some do," she agrees, giving a tight-lipped nod as if to imply this doesn't apply in her husband's case.

Mara's face softens, and for the first time, there's something almost vulnerable in her expression.

"There's only one Oscar," she says, as if that justifies everything carte blanche.

Even if I tried, I couldn't begin to understand the logic of a woman who has built her life around one complicated, controlling man.

"Can I tell you something?" She lowers her voice. "If I ever found Oscar's been talking to someone, I don't know what I'd do. But it wouldn't be pretty. And that kind of scares me because . . ."

Her words taper into nothing, though they still send a chill through me—not because I'm afraid of what she'd do if she found out I was talking to Oscar online, but because I would do the same thing if Will ever betrayed me. It would be primal, that urge. Coming from the deepest parts of me.

"No one's worth losing your freedom over," I tell her, snapping us both out of this.

Minka Kent

Mara chuckles. "Oh, you think I'd kill someone? No, no, no. I'm too pretty to go to prison."

I swallow and sit straight. Perhaps we're not as similar as I thought a moment ago.

"What would you do?" I ask.

"No idea. But I'd find a way to make life a little less enjoyable for them," she says. "They'd be sorry, that's for sure."

My mind conjures up a scenario where Oscar comes clean to Mara after the coffee shop incident earlier and the two of them are conspiring to bring me down—or inject a little discomfort into my "picture-perfect" life. It's impossible to know what anyone is capable of, but we're all capable of doing the unthinkable in extreme circumstances. People like me have more rein over their emotions because we don't feel them the way average people do. In a way, that makes people like them more dangerous. Like loose cannons. High emotions and impulsive actions are a dangerous and often deadly combination.

"Didn't Oscar's wife do that to you?" I ask.

"Yes," she says. "And it was awful. A special kind of hell I wouldn't put on anyone—unless they were trying to come between me and my husband. I think as women, we should reserve that right to protect what's ours."

Mara goes still, her expression unreadable until she leans back with a sigh, staring out at the water.

"Women tend to blame other women in these situations," I say. "I don't think that's always fair. I bet there are plenty of married men out there claiming to be single. Some of these women have no idea what they're getting into."

"Any woman who blindly dates someone these days without vetting them is an accomplice—unwitting or not. It's not hard to see if there's an indentation on their left finger, to do a search online and see where they reside and if they live with anyone."

"Some men give fake names," I say. "And some men are extremely charming and know all the right things to say. I'd be willing to go as far as to say they know exactly the type of woman who would fall for their tricks, too."

Mara rubs her lips together, contemplating something in silence—hopefully my perspective on this whole thing.

"I wish I didn't love him so much," she says under her breath, like a heartfelt confession. "It feels like a sickness sometimes. I need him. Even when he's at his worst."

"Pretty sure that's codependency," I tell her. "It's not healthy for either of you."

The juxtaposition of Mara waxing on about her love for her husband contrasts against my memory of Mara cozying up to Will at the party, fluttering those thick dark eyelashes, making him laugh in a way I haven't seen in months.

If she's so obsessed with her husband, why was she all over mine?

This isn't adding up.

Then again, with people as unstable as Mara, nothing ever does.

"Enough about Oscar," she says. "I feel like we've been talking about me this whole time. Tell me more about you and Will. You're like, I don't know, some sort of golden couple."

No denying that's the image we project.

"I think when you find the right person, it just works," I say. I refuse to give her so much as a single tidbit of information. She doesn't need to know the key ingredients to my proprietary marital recipe. No doubt she'd use them to her advantage if she ever had the opportunity.

"Well, that's boring," she teases. "What did you like most about him when you first met?" she asks. "What was your first impression? I *live* for these stories."

The afternoon light shifts, turning golden and soft. But before this conversation has a chance to get off the ground, the sound of the front door opening pulls me from my thoughts. Will steps out onto the patio a minute later, Jackson trailing behind him. Georgie skips close behind.

My perfect little family has perfect timing.

"Hey." Will grins when he spots us.

My dashing husband looks especially handsome today—dark khakis and a merlot-colored polo that clings in all the right places and makes his blue eyes appear bluer. He runs a hand through his salt-and-pepper temples, his eyes scanning the yard until they return to us.

Mara sits up a little straighter, her lips curving into a slow, deliberate smile. She unfastens her swimsuit wrap with a flick of her fingers, letting it fall off her hips to reveal her lithe, toned legs. The move is as obvious as it is intentional.

I catch a flicker of satisfaction in her eyes as Will's gaze shifts—just for a second—before he turns back to me. There's no sense of enjoyment on his face, much to my relief. If anything, he seems momentarily speechless.

Mara stretches her arms over her head, her bikini top shifting just enough to make her cleavage distractingly noticeable.

"I should probably get going," she says, standing slowly, as if reluctant to leave. She turns to me with a bright, dazzling smile that almost makes me forget all the things she was spouting out moments ago. "Thanks for having me over, Camille. We should do this again sometime."

I return the smile, though it takes a concerted amount of effort.

Mara reties her sheer wrap around her waist and waves as she heads toward the gate. "Great to see you, Will."

As she disappears down the path along the side of our home, I let out a slow breath, the tension in my shoulders refusing to ease.

"Everything okay?" He leans down to kiss my cheek. "I thought you said no more Morenos . . ."

"She invited herself over," I tell him.

"And you didn't say no?"

After the events of the day, I'm too mentally exhausted to think on my feet. No lies dance on the tip of my tongue, at least none that would be believable.

"She's not so bad," I eventually say, gathering up pool towels. "But I still think we should steer clear of them."

I hold my breath, waiting for Will to question me, to ask for an elaboration.

He doesn't.

18

"This is nice," Will says from the other side of our patio dining table. "We should do this more often."

The glow of the candlelight flickers between us, casting soft shadows across the tablespace. The hum of the night settles around us—the quiet buzz of crickets, the occasional rustle of leaves in the breeze, the faint sound of the pool filter running. The kids are finally asleep, leaving this sliver of time just for us.

It feels like a moment out of our previous life—before the doubts, the small cracks spreading beneath the surface. Before everything started shifting in ways I didn't anticipate.

Will pours the last of the wine into our glasses, his easy expression illuminated by the soft flame. He looks exceptionally good tonight—put together, in a charcoal button-down with the sleeves cuffed at his elbows, his dark hair catching the light. There's something calm and present about him tonight, as if it's just the two of us in our own little world.

And then I notice it—the sleek silver band circling his wrist.

"That's new," I say, gesturing toward the watch as I take a sip of wine.

Will glances down, turning his wrist slightly to admire it. "Oh, yeah. Just got this. It's vintage. Thought it looked classic. Looks good with my sport coats."

"What happened to your smartwatch? Did it break?"

He leans back in his chair.

"All the notifications were distracting in class. I'd be trying to explain something, and my wrist would be buzzing nonstop. It felt like I couldn't escape it. And when I'd turn off the settings, I'd always forget to turn them back on so it seemed pointless to even have it." He rubs the back of his neck. "This feels better. Simple. More me."

"More you?" I echo, turning the words over in my mind. "Lately, it feels like you're becoming someone else."

I didn't mean to say that out loud.

Or did I?

Will's good demeanor falters, just for a moment, but then his gaze turns soft and warm. "You say that like it's a bad thing. I thought you liked the way I've been dressing. You tell me how good I look every day."

I twirl the stem of my wineglass between my fingers, letting the silence stretch for a beat too long.

"You do look good," I assure him. "It's just . . . different. A lot of things feel different lately."

"We've gone through a lot of changes in a short amount of time. They're all good ones, though," he says. "Wouldn't you say? The kids are adjusting well. We're safe and happy. We've got everything we need. Maybe you're looking for something to worry about because for the first time in a long time, you don't have anything to worry about?"

I sniff, taking another sip.

If only *that* were the case.

Will leans forward, resting his elbows on the table, candlelight flickering in his dark eyes, silently willing me to meet his gaze.

"I like this fresh start for us," he says. "It feels good to let some things go."

I press my lips together, feeling the weight of the unspoken things between us.

"I liked what we had. It was perfect." I keep my voice even. "Until your mother came along and . . ."

The words dissipate between us, sharp and loaded but unspoken.

Will sighs, rubbing a hand across his five-o'clock shadow. "Camille . . ."

"It's true," I say, not bothering to soften the edges. I won't apologize for stating facts.

His mouth tightens, but he doesn't argue.

"*You* seem happier here," he says gently, changing the subject. "Unless you're pretending. You don't have to do that for me anymore, Camille. You don't have to be so perfect all the time. You can be . . . you."

He's referring to Gabrielle—my real name.

"I *am* being me," I tell him.

Will slices into his steak, which has long since cooled since we sat down. He chews a bite, his brows furrowing as his gaze grows unfocused.

"I miss how it used to be," I tell him. Everything was controlled, manageable. These days I'm mostly bored and feeling out of my element. It's as if something—or someone—has knocked me off balance and I've yet to regain my footing.

I used to be a step ahead of everyone, always, but now it seems there's nothing I can do to catch up.

The whole Oscar situation is proof of that.

Will leans back, appearing thoughtful. "Do you miss me working twenty-four-hour shifts at the hospital? Never being home to help with the kids? Hell, Camille, I was more married to my job than I was to you some weeks. I hated that. I hated that for you."

"We made it work."

"Do you want me to get a second job? Be gone more often?" His voice is light, teasing, but there's an edge beneath it—a challenge I'm not sure I'm ready to face.

"That's not what I mean." I roll my eyes and point my wineglass at him.

"Then what do you mean, Camille?" he asks, his voice low, calm. "What do you want? You miss how it used to be, but in which ways?"

I open my mouth to answer, but the words stick in my throat. I know exactly what I want—I want to know if he's having an affair. I want to know if Mara's flirtations mean something more. I want the truth, no matter how ugly it might be.

But I can't say that.

Part of me doesn't want to know yet—not until I have an idea of how I'd handle the worst-case scenario.

When I don't answer right away, concern flickers in his eyes.

"Are you doing okay?" His hand slinks across the table, covering mine. "Really, Camille. Are you doing okay?"

I swallow hard, forcing myself to smile.

"Of course," I say, though the lie tastes bitter on my tongue.

Will's chair scrapes against the patio floor as he stands and moves to sit beside me. He takes my hands in his, his touch warm and familiar.

"It's my job as your husband to make you happy." His thumb brushes gently over my knuckles.

I shake my head. "It's not fair to put it all on you. And I *am* happy. It'll just take some time to get used to everything."

"I don't think you are." He shifts closer, his gaze steady and sincere. "And if you're not happy, I'm not happy. Just tell me what you want. Whatever it is, I'll make it happen."

I stare at him, feeling the weight of his words settle over me. He means them—I know he does. And yet, there's a part of me that wonders if it's too good to be true. I've never questioned that before, but after briefly going down the rabbit hole of infidelity, it's become a lens through which I'm viewing my world.

"I'm fine." The lie slips out before I can stop it.

Will's brow furrows, and for a moment, he looks genuinely concerned. "You sure?"

"Yeah. I think I just need some time to adjust."

He watches me for a moment longer, his gaze searching mine, as if he's trying to find the truth buried beneath my words. Resigned, he sighs, squeezing my hand one last time before releasing it.

"Okay," he says softly. "But if there's anything you need from me, anything at all, let me know."

Will returns to his chair, watching me with an expression I can't quite read, and I wonder—just for a moment—if he knows exactly what I'm thinking.

If he does, he doesn't say.

And neither do I.

19

I was midway through folding a load of towels the following afternoon when Mara shows up at my door, dressed for the pool, a chilled bottle of wine in tow, uttering the words, "I could *kill* him."

Turning her away didn't feel like an option, so I slipped into my suit and met her out back.

The midday sun hangs high in the sky, the heat soaking into my skin as Mara and I lounge poolside. The sound of birds chirping and the occasional splash from the pool filter adds an oddly peaceful ambience to our strange little faux-friendship.

She leans back, sunglasses perched on her head, swirling the last bit of her wine in her glass. The bottle of pinot grigio sits on the concrete between us, gleaming in the sun like a silent witness to her unraveling.

"What happened?" I ask, even though I know the answer will be messy. Everything with Mara always is.

She exhales and reaches for the bottle, only to stop midway when she remembers it's already empty.

"I found a dating app on Oscar's phone this morning," she says flatly.

My stomach tightens. "What?"

"True Spark—the biggest one." She shifts in her chair, setting her glass down with a hollow clink.

"How?" My throat is dry, tight. This is either a setup or an eerie coincidence.

"He left his phone out while he was in the shower. It was unlocked, so I grabbed it." She nibbles on her french manicured nails, wincing as if she's a child about to get a verbal lashing for doing something naughty.

"And?" I ask.

She tips her head back and lets out a dry, humorless laugh. "He's been messaging *several* women on there. Not just one. Multiple."

"God. I'm so sorry." I feign shock as best I can, while also quelling my urge to panic. If she confronts Oscar and he finds out she's been spending time with me, he's going to assume I turned her on to this. There'll be no convincing him otherwise. "What did you do?"

"I deleted his entire account." She looks over at me, eyes wide with a mix of disbelief and fury. "Poof. Gone. Like it never existed. Then I deleted the app and blocked it in the App Store."

I let out a slow breath, bracing myself for the fallout. "Did he say anything?"

Mara snorts. "Not yet. I don't even think he's noticed because he hasn't said anything. He'll probably act like nothing happened. That's what he always does. He bottles it up and then makes me feel like I'm the one overreacting."

I stare out at the glimmering water, the sun reflecting off its surface in shimmering ripples. "What are you going to do?"

She tips her head back, draping an arm lazily over her eyes.

"Hang out here all day so I don't go home and accidentally murder him in a fit of rage." She laughs, but the dark flash in her blue eyes implies she might not be joking.

"Mara . . ." I say slowly, choosing my words. "You need to be careful. Remember what you said yesterday? You're too pretty to go to prison. And he's got a temper. You can't be so flippant about this stuff."

Mara lets out a bitter laugh, but her smile falters at the edges.

"Men like that aren't worth it," I continue, keeping my tone calm. "If he can't be loyal to you, why would you throw your life away for him? What do you get out of that?"

Mara's jaw tightens as she shifts in her chair, staring down at the pool water like it holds all the answers.

"It's not about what I get," she says.

"Then what's it about?"

"It's about proving a point." Her voice is low, almost too quiet to hear. "He promised he'd never cheat on me. He gave me his word. He knows how important this is to me. He knows it's the one thing that would destroy me."

"And he did it anyway." I offer her a hard truth but in the softest way possible. "You deserve better."

Comforting the woman I believe is crushing on my husband was not something I expected to be doing today—or ever, but I'm stuck for now.

"People break promises all the time," I say. "Especially people with a history of cheating."

Mara turns toward me, a flicker of defiance in her eyes. "It's not the same. He didn't leave his wife *for me*, he was about to leave her anyway. So technically, it wasn't cheating."

The logic twists in my mind, and I bite back the urge to argue.

Mara shifts her unsteady focus to the wine bottle, turning it slowly between her fingers before topping herself off—only she gets little more than a couple of drops. At the rate she's been guzzling, she's got to be drunk by now.

I watch her carefully, worried about what she'll do when the anger catches up to her. As impulsive as she is, I don't trust her not to storm back home and make a scene—or worse.

While I couldn't care less what Mara and Oscar do behind closed doors, I'd hate to wake up tomorrow to a scene of ambulances and cop cars filling our cul-de-sac. My children don't need to experience that again. Once was more than enough.

"So," she says, her voice deceptively casual. "What would you do if you found out Will was cheating?"

The question hits like a slap; sharp and sudden. My chest tightens as a dark thought flashes through my mind—violent and primal. I imagine grabbing Will by the throat, tearing him limb from limb, feeling his bones snap beneath my hands—which would never happen in real life. But in this fantasy, the thought is satisfying. It would only be fair.

If he broke up our happy home, I'd have no choice but to break him.

But the image is vivid, startling. I swallow hard, pushing it down, burying it beneath layers of control.

I appreciate my husband. I like what we have. I'd never want to harm him.

But if he betrays me, I can't promise I'd handle it with grace.

I don't do well with betrayal, with my world being threatened. Abusing my trust is something Lucinda lived for, the very thing I escaped. Being married to someone who'd do the same thing is something I could never subject myself to.

Mara is watching me closely now, waiting for an answer.

I force a small, tight smile. "I don't know. And I hope I never find out."

Mara cocks her head sideways, as if sensing there's more I'm not saying. But she lets it drop, leaning back in her chair with a sigh.

"Yeah," she says. "Me too. If Will ever cheats on you, there's no hope for anyone else. That man adores you. I can see it every time he looks at you. Reminds me of the way I look at Oscar." She glances down at her empty wineglass. "Well, before. I don't know how I'm going to look at him when I get home."

"What are you going to do about this?"

She lifts a shoulder to her ear. "What can I do? I deleted the app. I'll have to wait until he's in the right mindset before bringing it up or it could get ugly."

Ugly for everyone . . .

The sun shifts lower in the sky, casting long shadows across the patio. The air feels heavier now, weighed down by the things we've said—and the things we haven't.

As the sound of the front door opening drifts out to us, I glance toward the house. Will steps out onto the patio, carrying Jackson in one arm and Georgie trailing close behind. His easy, effortless smile spreads across his face as he spots us.

Mara shifts in her chair, sitting up straighter. Once again, with a casual, practiced motion, she unfastens her wrap and lets it fall away, revealing her toned, sun-kissed body in a sleek black bikini. The move is, once again, subtle but deliberate, her gaze flicking toward Will, as if she's mentally willing him to notice.

He doesn't so much as glance her way, at least not at first.

He's all about me, as he should be.

"Hey," Will says, his voice warm as he walks over to us. He gives me a quick kiss on the top of my head, then finally glances toward Mara with a polite smile. "Good to see you again, Mara."

Mara smiles, her eyes lingering on him a second too long. "You too, Will."

Tension coils in my chest, sharp and uncomfortable. I know what she's doing—she's testing my husband's loyalty, gauging where he directs his attention.

I stand, folding a striped pool towel under my arm.

"Thanks for coming over," I tell Mara, my voice chilled but polite. "We'll have to continue our conversation another time."

"Definitely," she says, moving to a lounge chair and lazily draping her wrap back over her thighs. She settles in, apparently not planning to go anywhere any time soon.

"Maybe tomorrow?" I suggest, but only because she's not getting the hint. I thanked her for her visit and folded my pool towel. My family is home. I'm not sure how any of this serves as an invitation for her to linger. There's nothing worse than an unwanted houseguest—except for maybe an unwanted houseguest who very much wants my husband.

"I need to start on dinner," I say, taking Will's hand and giving it a gentle squeeze. "Come help me in the kitchen?"

Will glances at me, a flicker of curiosity in his eyes, but he nods. "Of course."

Heading in, I glance back one last time at Mara, who's still lounging by the pool, her expression unreadable behind her giant sunglasses, though she's positioned in such a way that she's staring into the backside of our house—which is mostly comprised of floor-to-ceiling windows and sliding doors.

"She's sticking around?" Will asks, thumbing toward the pool.

"I guess," I say. "I think she needs some space from Oscar right now." I don't elaborate. The less I say, the better.

"So just to be clear," he says, "we need to steer clear of the Morenos, but it's okay if you drink wine with her by the pool?"

"Don't." I snip at him and I instantly regret it. "It's complicated. Woman stuff."

He shoots me a look as if I've insulted his emotional intelligence, and I know that I have.

"Marital issues. She thinks Oscar's cheating on her. I'll fill you in later," I say, though sharing this information with him feels like the wrong thing to do and for reasons I can't quite understand at the moment. "And I'm sorry for snapping at you. Mara's grating on my last nerves. I can't take another afternoon of being her free therapist."

Will moves behind me, massaging the tension from my shoulders before kissing the back of my head.

"I'll handle it," he assures me.

Turning to face him, I shake my head. "No. Don't. I don't want her to know I've shared any of this with you."

"You haven't really shared anything with me, though . . ."

He's not wrong. I pause. Before I have a chance to respond, Jackson and Georgie's screams trail in from the next room. I've never been so relieved to hear my children fighting over something.

"We'll talk about this later." I excuse myself from this conversation to tend to the children. When I'm finished, I return to Mara with my regrets, walk her to the side yard, and then I spend the rest of the afternoon avoiding Will at every turn.

I can't shake the feeling that this is all about to blow up in everyone's faces—and it's been a long time since I've felt so powerless.

I used to be the puppet master of our perfect little life, in control of each and every aspect.

Now? It's as if someone is cutting the strings one by one.

I need to get us back on course, whatever it takes.

20

Will's bathing the kids after dinner when I dodge out to grab the mail since it's been a minute. I suppose I've been avoiding it. Something tells me there's another Lucinda letter waiting for me.

Sure enough, I'm not wrong.

I open it the second I'm back inside. No sense in waiting.

This time, there's a photo included.

> My Gabrielle—
> I was clearing out some old storage bins when I came across your favorite childhood blanket—the one the nice lady from the Methodist church gave you when you were just a baby. You used to never let this out of your sight. It was the cutest thing. I used to wrap you up and rock you for hours. I miss the way you felt in my arms. I tried holding this blanket, but it wasn't the same. What I wouldn't give for another chance to hold you again. Motherhood is so fleeting and no one prepares you for the day your child says goodbye.

Heat flashes through me, though it dissipates quickly—as it always does. Feelings, even the primal ones, never last that long.

I'd almost forgotten about that blanket altogether, the ugly yellow and green chunky knit number that was laced with holes so big I could stick my fist through them. It barely kept me warm but sometimes it was all I had. Oftentimes, when money was tight, Lucinda would turn the thermostat down, dress herself in multiple layers, toss me the blanket, and tell me I had to "earn the rest of my warmth."

It was a game to her.

A game I could never win.

No matter what I did, it was never enough to earn warmth of any kind.

21

"Can't help but notice you've been spending a lot of time with Mara lately." The words come out of Sozi's mouth like a casual observation, but they're tinged with an undercurrent of something far less casual—jealousy.

"Ah, you noticed?" I ask.

The idea of Sozi standing on her second floor, peering out from behind a curtain, watching the neighborhood, creeps me out. Then again, she's mentioned many times how bored she is. It might be one of the most exciting parts of her day.

She shrugs, ponytail bouncing as we continue down the street. "Just in passing a couple of times."

"Mara's definitely interesting," I say. "Like you said. After everything you shared, I've decided I need to keep an eye on her."

"So you're being strategic."

"Something like that."

"Good. I think that's smart of you."

We walk in silence for a beat, the only sound the rhythm of our sneakers hitting the pavement—the usual soundtrack of our morning jaunts. I wait for her to say more, but the moment stretches just long enough to feel . . . strange.

"You're more than welcome to join us," I offer. "I was just under the impression you didn't like her."

"I like everyone," Sozi says. "I don't have anything against Mara. I just don't trust her around taken men is all."

I bite back a smile, pretending to be interested in the row of lavender bushes lining the sidewalk before shifting the conversation and nudging it toward safer ground.

"How's Austin? And Ezra?" I ask.

Sozi sighs, adjusting her pace to match mine. "Austin's the same. Work, golf, rinse, repeat."

"And Ezra?"

"Poor kid's allergies are brutal this time of year. He doesn't get outside much when it's like this."

"We should get the kids together soon. Finally make it happen."

"Absolutely. Once Ezra's breathing like a normal kid again, for sure. His asthma is just awful lately. It's like his inhaler isn't even doing anything for him. He sees his doctor in a couple of days, so I'll mention it, but I swear this happens every year. I think his allergies make it worse. Poor guy can't catch a break."

We lapse into a comfortable silence as we loop back toward my house, the morning sun warm on our backs. Once we reach my driveway, Sozi waves with her usual bright smile, her energy so effortless it almost makes me forget about the fact that she admitted to watching the comings and goings around my house.

I tell myself it could be a good thing. She'd tell me if anything was amiss.

I step inside my cool, quiet house and kick off my sneakers by the door. The air feels still, like the house has been holding its breath while I was gone. I head upstairs, stripping off my workout clothes as I go, already thinking about the shower I desperately need.

When I push open the door to the bedroom, the scent of Will's cologne lingers faintly in the air. It's that new one he's been wearing lately—clean, peppery, the kind of scent that clings just enough to make its presence known.

And then I see it.

Something shiny glinting on the dresser.

I walk closer, my steps slowing as the object comes into focus.

It's a necklace. A delicate gold chain with two small pendants in the shape of the letters *M* and *O*.

Mara's necklace.

My stomach tightens, my pulse ticking faster as I stare down at it. Mara was wearing this the day we had coffee, but I don't recall her wearing it by the pool yesterday.

What the hell is it doing in my bedroom?

I run through various possibilities, but none of them make sense. Will never mentioned anything about Mara being in here, and I've never invited her in. We always go around the side of the house, through the back gate.

I hover my hand over the necklace, but I don't touch it. My mind spirals, turning over every possibility, each one more unsettling than the last.

Did she leave it here on purpose? Did Will put it here?

Or—

This doesn't belong here. It shouldn't be here. And yet, it is.

I rake it into my palm and place it in my top dresser drawer, with the rest of my jewelry, until I can ask Will about it later.

For his sake, I hope he has a perfectly logical explanation.

22

"Where's the stinky cheese?" Jackson waves his spaghetti-covered fork around like a baton, making a mess on the table.

Georgie rolls her eyes dramatically, the way only a kindergartner can. "It's called *parmesan*."

"On the counter, Jack-Jack," Will says, pushing his chair back to grab it. He sets the green canister down in front of Jackson with a wink, ruffling his hair. "There you go."

We're halfway through dinner when the knock comes—a sharp, insistent rap at the front door.

I look up at Will and am met with a frown. We don't get many visitors, especially not this late. And whoever's at the door took it upon themselves to bypass our driveway gate. The kids pause, their chatter dying down as Will wipes his hands on his napkin and stands.

"I'll get it," he offers.

He heads for the door, and soon the low murmur of voices trails down our entrance hall—Will's steady tone, the other tense and urgent. When he returns to the dining room, Oscar Moreno is right behind him.

Oscar's face is pale, his hair disheveled like he's been raking his hands through it over and over. His eyes dart around the room, focused and unfocused, before landing on me.

This can't be good.

I feel it in my marrow, raw and pulsing.

"Camille," Oscar says, his voice rough and shaky, "I haven't seen Mara since yesterday. She was gone when I got home from work and she didn't come home last night. She's not answering her phone. Her location's off. Her car's in the garage. I thought . . . I thought maybe she was upset with me about something . . . I thought she just needed to cool off and maybe went to grab drinks with a friend but now that I haven't heard from her, I'm starting to get worried. This isn't like her."

My stomach tightens. "What do you mean?"

Oscar pulls at his hair again, pacing a few steps before stopping abruptly.

Rising from my seat, I hook my hand into the bend of his elbow and lead him into the kitchen. Will follows. My children don't need to witness this—whatever it is.

He looks like a man dangling on the edge of panic, a man whose world is two seconds from caving in. "It's not like her."

I swallow hard, keeping my voice steady. "Mara was here yesterday afternoon, she left around four. I assumed she went home after that. I haven't heard from her."

Oscar's expression crumples, and for a split second, I catch a glimpse of something distorted and unnerving—as if he suspects *I* had something to do with this.

I fold my hands in front of my hips, maintaining an air of calm composure while internally, my mind is spinning, trying to work the pieces together. Did Mara run off to teach Oscar a lesson, or did she confront him and he snapped?

He's a desperate man with a temper and secrets. He could easily be playing the part of a grieving husband. Setting the stage for the act about to unfold.

"We'll keep an eye out," Will says, his voice assuring and steady, as if none of this is of grave concern to him—which is slightly concerning to me. He's almost too collected. "Let us know if you hear anything."

Oscar gives a jerky nod, looking like he's barely holding it together. His lower lip quivers. If I didn't know him from Adam, I'd think he was genuinely worried something happened to her. But people lie all the time. And if he's like me, he can turn on waterworks without much effort.

"I'd appreciate that. Sorry to bother you guys in the middle of dinner." Oscar turns and walks out, but not before casting one last, frantic glance toward the street, as if hoping Mara will suddenly appear from the shadows.

When the door clicks shut behind him, I exhale and turn toward Will. My mind goes to Mara's pendant, the one I found in our bedroom earlier today. I was planning to mention it to Will later tonight, after the kids go to bed.

"Do you think something happened to her?" I ask.

Will's head jerks toward me, his eyes wide, just as clueless as me. "God, I hope not."

He runs a hand through his hair, a familiar streak of worry lines forming above his brow. "Maybe she went to a hotel or something. You said they've been having marital issues. People do that when they need space," he says.

"I don't know. She mentioned to me she thinks her husband is talking to other women and then she . . . vanishes without a trace that very same night? And Oscar waits a whole day to tell us he can't find her?"

"I'm not disagreeing with you. It's all very suspicious." He walks over to the tablet we use for our home security system and pulls up the camera feed. "Let's see if the cameras caught anything. Do we have a view of their house?"

I shake my head. "Just the edge of their driveway gate, but with all the shrubs, there's nothing to see."

He taps through the feed, but just as I said, there's nothing—only shadows and an empty street. He sighs, setting the tablet back on the counter.

"You're not still planning to go golfing with Oscar on Friday, are you?" I ask, my tone sharper than I intended.

Will turns to me, head cocked at my admittedly stupid question. "Obviously not if Mara's still missing."

The unspoken aspects of the situation claw at the back of my throat—the dating app, the messages Oscar sent me, all wiped away now like they never existed, the confrontation at the coffee shop. All secrets that've disappeared into thin air, leaving nothing but questions in its place, and now there's a missing neighbor's necklace in our bedroom.

At the end of the day, the equation is quite simple: I was catfishing her husband on a dating app, she was flirting with mine at a party, her necklace mysteriously made its way to our bedroom, and now she's missing.

The whole thing is uncomfortably intertwined.

But I can't tell Will any of that.

Because if he *is* involved with Mara, he can't know that I'm onto him. Not yet.

23

"I found this on the dresser today." I hold up Mara's delicate gold chain, the two charms catching the soft glow of the bedside lamp. Will glances up from his book, blinking like he's been pulled from a dream, his brow furrowing as he focuses on the chain dangling from my hand.

I wasn't going to say anything, but I got a wild hair earlier and decided to test his reaction. His reaction should let me know if this is something innocuous . . . or damning.

He sits up a little, resting his back against the headboard. "Yeah, I left it there for you. It must've fallen off your neck at some point. Georgie found it in the driveway."

"It's not mine." I display the initials, holding them flush against the palm of my hand. "*M* and *O*. Mara and Oscar. It's her necklace. I've seen it on her before."

"Ah, okay. Guess I didn't look that closely. I just saw two sparkly shapes." He shrugs, the movement easy and natural, like he's talking about a stray sock. "Georgie brought it to me because she thought it looked fancy, and I figured it might be yours. Didn't want to risk her running off with it in case it was expensive. You know how she's been into jewelry lately."

"You don't think it's weird?"

He gives me an endearing look. "It probably fell off when she was going between our house and hers."

"Mara was wearing it the other day when she was here. I could see it being in the side yard, but how would it end up in our driveway?"

Will shrugs again, handing the necklace back to me. "These things happen. Maybe it slipped off without her noticing. No sense in reading into it."

I roll the gold letters between my thumb and forefinger, my mind racing. "What do we do with it?"

"Nothing." He leans back, propping his arms behind his head. "It's just a necklace. It's not some missing clue that's going to tell us where she is."

The words sit between us, heavy and strange, but his tone is calm—too calm, like there's nothing about any of this that's bothering him.

"And who knows, she might even be home by now." He glances at the clock on the nightstand. It's late. Almost 11:00 PM. If she did come home, Oscar wouldn't likely bother us with the news at this time of night.

I survey my husband, trying to find a flicker of something—guilt, suspicion, recognition. But Will looks exactly the same as always: calm, practical, and reasonable.

Completely unbothered.

"It's *just* a necklace," he reminds me softly, brushing his hand over mine.

Exhausted, I rest the pendant on my nightstand, but the knot in my stomach tightens. He seems so completely clueless yet utterly convincing at the same time, and there's no denying his explanation is perfectly logical.

The necklace glints faintly under the lamplight, and I wonder—if it's just a necklace, why can't I stop thinking about it?

24

Will's phone rests screen side up on the nightstand, taunting me as he takes his morning shower.

I couldn't sleep last night.

For eight hours, my mind did nothing but race, coming up with a hundred scenarios, some of which were upsettingly plausible.

Holding my breath, I dive for his phone, tap in the passcode, and pull up his messages. It takes a bit of scrolling, but I stop the instant I find a text thread between Will and someone only entered into his phone as "M."

Every muscle in my body twists, hot and searing, as I pull up the texts. The most recent one, sent a handful of days ago from Will, is a simple: I miss you.

The rest of the messages between them are damning, almost all of them sent from "M."

. . . do you love the cologne?

. . . I bet the watch looks amazing on you.

. . . I love you so much.

. . . It pains me that we can't be together right now.

. . . When do you think we can meet up?

. . . Call me on your lunch break today.

I don't have a chance to write down the phone number before the shower shuts off. Darkening his screen, I return his phone back to its spot on the nightstand and walk away before I do something I can never undo.

25

"Oscar?" His name slips out before I realize it, my voice cutting through the still night air as I pad across our driveway and cut through the side yard that leads to the Morenos'.

He's sitting on the top step, a whiskey glass dangling loosely from his hand, shoulders hunched like the weight of the world is pressing down on him. His hair is a mess, and his eyes are bloodshot, the kind of exhaustion you can't sleep off.

He looks up slowly, and for a moment, I wonder if he's too drunk to recognize me. But then his lips curve into a sad, familiar shape—something between a smile and a grimace.

"Camille," he slurs my name.

The smell of whiskey drifts toward me, mixing with his unfocused gaze.

"She's been gone for *days*." His voice cracks slightly, dragging my attention back to him. "This isn't normal."

I sit down on the step beside him, the cool concrete pressing against my legs. "Did you contact the police yet?"

He nods slowly, his eyes fixed on some point far down the street.

It's been two days since I found those texts between Will and "M." Yesterday I managed to get the phone number when he wasn't looking, only it was a Google number. Not linked to anyone. Virtually untraceable unless you're law enforcement. While it would be easy to throw Will under the bus right now, until I know exactly what's going on and what I intend to do about it, I'm keeping this information to myself. The last thing I want is to get implicated in something I've got nothing to do with.

"Yeah. Filed a report this morning. They asked the usual questions." He swirls the whiskey in his glass.

"What about your security cameras?" I point toward the one mounted by the garage.

A bitter laugh escapes his thin lips.

"Battery was dead in the driveway camera. Just my luck, right?" He takes another drink, the melting ice clinking softly against the glass. "They said they'd check with the neighbors, see if anyone else caught anything. Have they asked you guys?"

"Not yet."

I watch him carefully. I'm not convinced this is an act anymore. Gone is the ominous, threatening Oscar I met in the coffee shop last week. The man before me looks defeated, downtrodden, weak.

"You think something happened to her?" I keep my tone gentle. "Or do you think she left on her own?"

Oscar's breath hitches as he rubs his hands over his face, his wedding band catching on his stubble.

"I hope she left on her own because if something happened to her . . ." He drags in a shaky breath. "I don't know what I'd do."

I study him, his slumped posture, the way he grips his glass like it's the only thing keeping him grounded.

Lucinda was a fine actor. Any problem she presented, any emotion she displayed, felt undeniably authentic to those who didn't know the woman who lurked behind her many masks. I don't know Oscar well enough to categorize him as another Lucinda, but until Mara is found, I'd be stupid to rule anything out.

"Mara seems intensely loyal to you," I say, careful to keep my tone neutral. "And very forgiving. If she left on her own accord, I'm sure she'll come back."

Oscar lets out a derisive snort I can't interpret.

He drains the rest of his whiskey and shakes his head.

I lean back slightly, pressing my arms around my knees. "It's not my place, but . . . what's your relationship really like? I heard Mara's version, but it seems to be a little different from your perspective. I'm trying to understand the dynamic."

Oscar shoots me a sideways glance, suspicion flickering in his eyes. "What are you, some kind of marriage counselor? What are your qualifications, exactly?"

"Just a nosy neighbor," I say with a small smile, trying to keep things light. In all seriousness, I add, "And someone who has a keen way of observing things about people. I notice things most people don't. Since I don't know either of you that well, I was hoping you could fill in some blanks. Maybe I'll be able to add a more objective angle to all of this for you. Or I can at least try."

He huffs, shaking his head. "Sorry. That was a dick thing to say."

Staring into his empty glass, he's lost in thought for a moment. Then his lips press flat. "I think she was talking to someone else."

The knot in my stomach grows painfully tight. "Why do you think that?"

He leans forward, elbows resting on his knees.

"I caught her cheating on me not too long ago. I didn't say anything because I wasn't quite sure yet what I was going to say. It's not the first time and she would've denied it anyway. So I guess in an attempt to make myself feel better, I went on that stupid dating app a couple weeks ago." His voice is low, edged with shame. "Honestly, I just wanted to get back at her. It felt good, knowing I still could if I wanted to. I wasn't going to date anyone."

I sit quietly, letting the weight of his words settle between us. He says that—but he still showed up.

"The day she disappeared, she must've seen the app on my phone," he says. "Because I realized later that day, it had been deleted. The whole damn account, just like that. I don't know what would've possessed her to even look at my phone that day . . . do you?"

The night air is heavy, thick with unspoken truths. I shift, uncomfortable on the concrete step.

"I know what you're implying," I say. "But you couldn't be more wrong."

Rising, he staggers to his front door, shooting me a look I can only describe as drunken indifference.

Still, it chills me to the bone.

26

"Did you see it? The news report on Mara?" Sozi's ponytail swings as we walk, energy crackling off her like static.

I tug my sweatshirt over my head, the morning air cool against my cheeks. "Yeah. I couldn't believe how brief it was."

"Six days," she says, more to herself than to me. "People don't just vanish like that. Not unless they want to . . . or not unless someone wants them to."

The words hang heavy between us.

Six days.

No texts.

No calls.

No sightings beyond the gate.

Mara's missing, but Phoenix is a place where news has the lifespan of a fruit fly. The city has already moved on, distracted by another hit-and-run, a fire downtown, a local celebrity caught in a scandal. Mara's face—smiling, oblivious—only appeared on the TV screen for a few hours before it was replaced by something shinier. The article posted on the news station website is already buried by sixteen other articles and a variety of flashing internet ads.

We walk in silence for a block, the rhythm of our steps falling into sync.

If the "M" in Will's phone is Mara, she hasn't texted him in six days—a damning coincidence. But also, if Will were having an affair, what reason would he have to kidnap or murder her? It's extreme and unnecessary and the antithesis of who Will is at his core.

Then again, he's a product of Jacqueline.

And Jacqueline had us all fooled.

"I feel like she'll be back," Sozi says, though her words lack confidence. "I bet she'll have one hell of a story to tell, too. It'll all make sense."

"Is that what you believe or is that what you want to believe?"

"A little of both maybe."

It's quiet again, and we stride past another block of sprawling ranches in silence.

I haven't made love to Will in several days—not since I found the text messages. He tried the other night, but I turned him down for the first time ever, told him I'm too worried about Mara to get into the mood. He let it go. I've been emotionally distant since. Another thing I'm blaming on Mara. He's buying it for now, though I'm not sure how much longer I can string this along. I can pretend with the best of them, it's what I do, but I draw the line at betrayal.

He doesn't deserve me.

It isn't until we round the corner when Sozi clears her throat. "You know, I wasn't sure if I should mention it, but I saw Will talking to Mara outside the night before she went missing. Not trying to imply anything. I'm sure it's just a coincidence. But I wanted to say something."

The words feel like a sudden drop in temperature, cutting through the morning air. I glance at her, trying to keep my expression neutral.

She pulls her phone from her jacket pocket. "Here. I took a couple of pictures. I know that's weird, I just . . . I know how Mara is and I guess I wanted to document it in case she ever made a move on Will. You know me—too much time on my hands."

She hands me her cell, and my stomach cinches as I scroll through the photos. There, in the grainy light of the streetlamps, is Will—standing by the end of our driveway. And there's Mara, her body tilted toward his, her face too shadowed to read. They aren't touching, but they're close. Closer than I'd have been comfortable with had I been there.

My fingers curl tighter around the phone. I hand it back before I shatter it in my palm.

Sozi shrugs, sliding the phone into her pocket. "It's odd. Isn't it?"

"Odd," I echo, the word sticking like a splinter.

She gives me a look I can't quite read. "Oh, God. Should I not have shown you those?"

"No," I say. "It's just . . ."

I trail off, unsure how to finish the sentence. It's just that I want to scream. It's just that I feel like the ground beneath my feet is starting to shift, pulling me toward something I don't want to see. It's just that the life I've worked so hard to create for my family was built on a foundation of lies designed to keep them safe. If Will is having an affair with Mara, if Will has something to do with this . . .

We turn another corner, the blacktop street stretching out in front of us, lined with the same pristine houses, the same trimmed hedges and raked rock yards. Any other day, the perfection would be par for the course. Today it's as if I've entered some kind of twilight zone.

None of it feels real.

"I'm not saying they were having an affair or anything," Sozi says. "But people don't meet outside late at night for no reason."

The sun peeks over the horizon, casting long shadows along the sidewalk. I glance toward our house, my heart pounding a little harder than it should be.

"Anyway," Sozi says, glancing at her watch. "I better get back. Ezra's got a Zoom lesson in half an hour, and I need to make sure Austin didn't forget to unmute the mic again."

We part ways at my driveway, but all of her words linger, curling around my thoughts like smoke.

As I slip back inside the house, I pull my phone from my pocket, scrolling absently through the missed notifications.

Nothing from Mara.

Nothing from Will.

And still no answers—only more questions.

I head upstairs, the house eerily quiet until Will's voice drifts faintly from the bedroom—he's on a call for work, the low hum of professional charm. I pause in the hallway, the photos on Sozi's phone playing in my mind like some highlight reel.

Will and Mara. Late at night. Talking.

Talking about what?

The fact is, they shouldn't have been talking at all. If I ask him about it, he'll likely lie, make up something harmless. And at the end of the day, what they were talking about doesn't matter—it's the fact that he was talking to her at all, knowing damn well that he wasn't supposed to, and then failed to mention any of it to me.

The whole thing is a middle finger to our marriage.

A cold knot twists in my gut, and I shove the thought away before it can fully take root. There has to be an explanation. There always is. But the thing about explanations is—they don't always come when you need them.

Will is an intelligent man. If he had anything to do with Mara's disappearance, he's got to be ten steps ahead of me by now.

I reach for the bedroom door handle before stopping halfway.

I need my questions answered, but more important than that, I need to strategize.

27

"Why did you get this cologne, by the way?" I ask Will, nodding toward the amber, phallic-shaped bottle sitting on our dresser. Will has always been a classic man. I can't imagine him choosing this on his own.

Will glances up from where he's folding a shirt, one brow slightly raised, as if the question surprises him. "The cologne?"

"Yeah." I lean against the doorframe, keeping my voice light. "I meant to ask the other week."

He smiles, his expression easy. "Stopped at the mall with Jackson one day and they were handing out free samples at one of the department stores. I liked it, so I went back the next day and bought a bottle."

I study his face, searching for cracks in the story, but everything about him is as calm and sincere as ever. I don't recall him mentioning taking Jackson to the mall recently, but we don't tend to share every minute detail of our days.

"The saleswoman said it was new," he continues, tossing the folded shirt into a drawer. "Apparently they can hardly keep it in stock. Must be popular. I think she said it went viral online or something."

Everything about his story makes perfect sense—except it's almost too perfect.

He turns to me, a playful grin tugging at the corners of his mouth. "Why? Don't you like it anymore?"

The question feels innocent, the tone affectionate, but it only tautens the knot of suspicion in my chest. It's such a reasonable explanation, the kind you can't argue with—which makes me trust it even less.

"No, it's not that," I say. "I was just curious."

Will's gaze lingers on me for a moment longer, almost as if he's ascertaining whether my question was truly genuine, then he closes the dresser drawer with a soft thud.

"Are you going into work today?" I ask.

He shakes his head.

"It's a professional development day. Webinars all afternoon." He drinks me in, dipping his life-saving hands into his pockets. "I figured I'd do them here, in the comfort of my living room, my beautiful wife close by."

"Still want me to come by and decorate your office sometime?" My question is more of a test than an offer.

His handsome grin widens. He steps closer, slipping his hands around my waist.

"I'd love nothing more." Will leans in to kiss the tip of my nose. "Come by any time you want."

"Ooh, an open invitation?" I tease, testing him more.

"You have a permanent standing open invitation."

I've spent so many years tiptoeing around his hospital shifts, carefully constructing my day around his unpredictable schedule. This version of Will—the one who works reasonable hours, the one who invites me into his professional life—feels foreign.

"A girl could get used to this," I tell him, which elicits a twinkle in his eye—the same one I've been seeing more than ever lately. If he were having an affair, though, I don't think he'd give me a *permanent standing open invitation* to his office.

Except, of course, if his affair partner was out of the picture.

He kisses my forehead, his lips warm and soft. I leave my body for a moment.

"Good. Get used to it," he whispers. "I want you there. I want to see you as much as possible. You're my favorite person in the world,

Cam. Our whole marriage, I've worked long hours and left you alone far more than I should have. It's a miracle you've stuck it out. If I haven't said it enough, I'm grateful for everything you do for our family."

His words linger, sinking into the hairline fissures that have formed between us.

Will releases me and grabs his laptop from the nightstand, propping it open on the bed.

"How was your walk with Sozi?" he asks over his shoulder. "Any new developments with Mara?"

I hesitate, weighing how much to tell him. "Nothing."

Will scans his fingerprint, unlocking his MacBook.

"What's your theory?" I ask.

He exhales slowly, as if the question itself weighs too much, and he turns his gaze toward the window despite the curtains being drawn.

"I don't want to begin to guess. It could be anything." He looks at me, his gaze steadier now, in focus. "Honestly, I'd rather not think about it. It has nothing to do with us."

I disagree.

And interesting choice of words.

"So, we might be living next door to a murderer and you're just going to bury your head in the sand?" I cross and then uncross my arms. I'm not trying to put him on the defense, but his attitude about this is too casual for my comfort.

Will straightens, his expression turning serious. "You think Oscar killed her? Is that your theory?"

"Statistically," I keep my voice measured, "when a woman goes missing or ends up dead, it's more often than not at the hands of her romantic partner."

My words are a test.

Will nods slowly, his expression unreadable. "This is true."

He reaches for me and takes my hand, bringing it to his lips but not kissing it, almost as if he forgot to complete the move because his mind is elsewhere.

"We can talk more about this after my seminars." His thumb brushes over my knuckles.

The warmth of his touch, the familiar weight of his affection—it should make me feel safe. And for a fleeting moment, it does. But beneath his warm gestures, something cold lingers. A nagging doubt I can't quite shake.

I squeeze his hand before letting it go. "Sounds good."

As I turn to leave the room, the scent of his cologne catches me again, trailing after me like whispered secrets.

28

Lucinda's letters are arriving with almost a maddening frequency now. She's up to something, though I've yet to determine what it is. She's made it clear she knows where I live and that I'm living under an alias. She's rewriting history as a way to get under my skin and remind me of the torment I lived through a lifetime ago. But nothing can prepare me for today's letter.

My Gabrielle—

I think of you often, if you can believe it. There isn't a day that goes by that I wish things had been different between us. I often look at other mothers and daughters and wonder how it might have been had our circumstances been more conventional. There are things I've never shared with you—things that might provide the context I'm sure you've always needed. While it's too late to change the past and wishing things were different is a waste of time that I don't have (more on that another day), I hope you can take solace in knowing I'm a much better mother to your half sister than I was to you.

If we never meet again, I wanted you to know you have a sister. She's thirteen and she's got your hazel-brown eyes and wide smile. I see a little bit of you in her every single day. In another life, the two of you would have a wonderful bond. I just know it.

> She knows nothing about you or your existence, and while you don't owe me anything, the mother I was and the other I now am might as well be strangers and I ask that you keep it that way—not for me but for her.

Lies.

I refuse to believe any of it.

I shove the letter in the drawer with the others and go about my morning. But curiosity gnaws at me for hours. Lucinda painting herself as a saint of a mother is something she was always good at, but I know her better.

If I truly do have a sister, she could be in grave danger.

Flipping the envelope over, I inspect the postmark on the back.

Hinsdale, Illinois.

If I recall, Hinsdale is an upscale Chicago suburb, a place with new money and old, tree-lined streets with million-dollar mansions. Clearly she's still in the greater Chicago area. And driving out of her way to mail letters from a specific post office is something Lucinda wouldn't hesitate to do.

Once again, her motives have me perplexed. Emotional whiplash. Mental torment. But to what end? And why now?

Taking the letters from the drawer, I reread them, poring over them once again.

If a stranger read them, if they were taken at face value, Lucinda would seem like a remorseful mother, her letters reading like pseudo-apologies. Even if they were, it's too little, too late. She can't undo a lifetime of trauma and abuse with a few "heartfelt" letters.

I shove the letters back into their spot, still unsure what to make of them.

The only thing I know for sure is that Lucinda might as well be dead to me.

29

"Mara's home." Sozi stands at my front door shortly before lunchtime, shell-shocked and breathless, her hair sticking out in every direction, as if she forgot to run a brush through it before dashing over here to tell me the news.

Her words make my heart come to a hard stop.

By the time I slip on my sandals and step out the front door, Sozi's already pacing the sidewalk, her phone clutched in one hand. She glances up as I approach, eyes wide with a mix of disbelief and excitement.

"A police car dropped her off a little bit ago," Sozi says. "Like, not even ten minutes ago. Oscar's home, too. What do you think happened?"

"I don't know," I say, still wrapping my head around the news.

We both peer at the Morenos' home, where the heavy driveway gate is closed tight this time. Their house sits in perfect stillness, but now there's a weight to it—like a storm cloud that hasn't quite burst.

"You think we should go over and knock?" Sozi chews her lip. "I mean, just to check in. See if everything's okay?"

I hesitate, biting the inside of my cheek. The thought of facing Mara after all the guessing, the suspicion, the fear . . . makes my skin crawl. But curiosity itches at me, too, sharp and relentless.

"Maybe we should wait," I say. "Give them space. Let them . . . settle."

Sozi chuffs but doesn't argue. "I guess. But still—what the hell happened?"

I shake my head, my mind whirring with unanswered questions. The last time anyone saw Mara, she was unraveling at the seams, and now she's back, escorted home by a patrol car. While we both want answers, we're not entitled to them. I hardly know Mara, and Sozi is more of a bona fide nosy neighbor than close friend.

"I'm going to call Will," I announce.

Sozi raises an eyebrow, though she doesn't share her thoughts. At this point, I don't want to know. The last thing I need is more of her conjecture. She all but implied Will and Mara were having an affair and that he might have had something to do with Mara's disappearance the other day. While I appreciated her taking the photos, I didn't appreciate her offering them as proof of anything other than two neighbors talking. It felt a little . . . *much.*

Sozi has her nose to the ground around here, but she doesn't have the gift of discernment.

Not everything is *something.*

I step away from her, dialing Will's number. The phone rings . . . and rings . . . and rings, before finally clicking over to voice mail.

"Of course," I sigh under my breath.

I could use a change of scenery, a break from Sozi, the Morenos, and Saguaro Circle, and Will said I had an open standing invitation to his office, so my next move is a no-brainer. Plus, I want to see the look on his face when I tell him the news in person.

"I've got some errands to run. I'll catch you later," I tell Sozi before heading to grab my car keys.

By the time I'm backing out of my driveway a few minutes later, Sozi is perched on her front steps, watching the Moreno house so intently she doesn't even notice when I wave.

30

"Can I help you?" A silver-haired woman with an abundance of turquoise jewelry greets me with a friendly, lifted expression. While her face is smiling, her eyes curiously scan me from head to toe.

"I'm Camille Prescott—Will's wife," I say.

"Oh!" She claps her hands together. "Yes, I remember seeing you about a month or so ago. How have you been?"

I don't recall seeing her when I was here last time, but I keep that to myself.

"Great. I was hoping Will was around?" I stay on task.

"He's in with a student right now. You're welcome to have a seat and wait." She points to a couple of waiting room chairs, silver metal upholstered in maroon bouclé—a nod to school colors.

There's a section of window next to his office door where the blinds have not been drawn closed. From here, I can spot him. Part of him, anyway. He's standing behind his desk, talking to someone who, based on their lithe arm and red nail polish, is a female student.

My mind goes to the texts between Will and "M."

What if "M" wasn't Mara? What if "M" was a student? It would make sense, the way he's taking his new career in education as an excuse to give himself a complete makeover. There's no denying he's exactly the kind of professor the young girls would lose their minds over, much like the nurses did at the hospitals where he once worked.

I never thought I needed to worry.

I gave him everything he could ever want and more.

My foot is tapping. The receptionist glances over. I stop and cross my legs.

Eight minutes later, his door swings open. The student—young, pretty, with a slick-backed platinum ponytail—gives him a finger wave and a few thank-yous before tucking a thick file under her arm. When she passes on her way out, she leaves me in a cloud of overdone perfume and cinnamon chewing gum.

"Camille." The instant Will notices me, his whole face lights. "Isn't this a nice surprise? Wasn't expecting to see you here."

I'm sure he wasn't . . .

He ushers me in and shuts the door behind us. Taking a seat on the edge of his desk, he reaches for my waist and pulls me close. Never mind that the blinds are still open on one of his windows. I place my hands over his to temper his intentions, whatever they may be.

Now is not the time.

His office is smaller than I remember, and the air smells faintly of old coffee and printer paper, the walls bare except for a framed degree and a couple of dry-erase boards cluttered with half-finished notes in his impossibly illegible handwriting.

I can smell the faint, sweet scent of a cinnamon-perfume cocktail in the space I now share with my husband. It bothers me more than it should.

Will, for his part, seems unbothered, oblivious.

Knowing what I now know, I'm convinced it's an act—a page out of his mother's playbook.

"I tried calling you." I brush off his second attempt to pull me closer.

"Had my phone on silent. I was with a student." He shrugs, his hands still lingering on my sides. "Can I help you with something, Mrs. Prescott? Or are you just here to see me?"

His charm is disarming. I'll give him that. But today it repels me.

I push his hands away, gently but firmly. "Mara came home."

"You're kidding. That's great. I figured she would." His expression is one of pleasant surprise, but his reaction is still too easy, too light—as if we're talking about the weather, not the neighbor whose face was plastered across the news just days ago.

"You don't seem that interested."

"Wouldn't it be strange if I cared . . . too much?" He blinks slow, the corners of his mouth still curled in that infuriatingly calm grin.

I fold my arms. "I don't get how you can act like it's nothing."

He lets out an exasperated sigh, running a hand through his hair and leaving a disheveled trail in its wake. "I feel like I can't do anything right lately. If I care too much, that's a problem. If I don't care enough, that's also a problem. What exactly do you need from me? How can I make you happy again?"

He's playing the victim, but I see through it.

He knows exactly what he's doing.

He's no idiot, though I'm beginning to wish he were.

Two can play this game—but only one of us will win.

I glance toward the window, the late-morning sun slanting through the blinds in neat stripes.

"I don't know anymore." The words slip out before I can stop them. "Nothing has felt right since we moved to Saguaro Circle."

Will leans back against his desk, arms crossed over his expanding chest. He watches me closely, as if waiting for something more. "Are you saying you want to move?"

I think about the location—the privacy. The security. The gates upon gates. The cameras. The quiet, cloistered neighborhood that felt like a sanctuary when we first arrived.

Now it just feels like a prison.

Will's desk phone rings, the receptionist announcing another student is waiting for him in the lobby.

He winces, apologetic. "I hate to leave you like this, but I have another appointment. Can we finish this talk tonight?"

I pause, giving him a sullen, sad-eyed look, and then I nod like the loyal, trusting, agreeable wife he wants to believe I still am. After everything that came to light in San Diego, I never changed who I was around him or how I treated him. I stayed the same. I had to. It was the only way to keep our marriage intact. Jacqueline had already tried to ruin it—I wasn't going to give her the pleasure of knowing it crumbled anyway.

While Will is busy pulling up files on his computer, I swipe his phone off the credenza behind him and tuck it into my pocket. "See you tonight."

31

I'm halfway home when I can't take the suspense another minute. I pull off into a Whole Foods parking lot and retrieve Will's phone out of my bag. Scrolling through his texts, I find the thread between him and "M."

Sure enough, there was a message from "M" sent yesterday— Thinking of you always, my love. Wish we were together right now, but I know we will be soon. I truly hope your wife can someday understand and forgive me and we can all leave the past in the past.

I see red.

Then everything goes black.

32

"Camille." Mara leans against the frame of her front door, arms crossed, her blond waves draped over one shoulder. She looks exhausted in all the ways and thinner than ever, like she left a piece of herself wherever she was the last several days. But her expression is composed, carefully neutral, like she's trying to act like everything's fine. "I wasn't expecting you."

I came straight here as soon as I got home from picking up groceries. Didn't even bother unloading them. Until I know if "M" is Mara, nothing else matters.

"I heard you were back. I wanted to personally stop by and tell you I'm glad you're home safe. You had us all worried." I study her in better detail, scanning her expression for guilt, shock, a confirmation that she's a giant piece of home-wrecking shit.

"Thank you," she says, her voice low, laced in shame or secrecy perhaps.

"Is everything okay?" I ask. "With you and Oscar? Are *you* okay?"

While I feign compassion, I'm merely gathering information.

She rolls her eyes. "I'm fine. I was . . . I wasn't acting rationally. After finding the dating app on his phone, I wanted to retaliate, I guess. I wanted him to know he could lose me. I thought disappearing would make him panic, make him regret it. It was impulsive and childish, I know. But at the time? It felt . . . like my best option. Again,

I wasn't thinking straight. I'm honestly pretty embarrassed about the whole thing."

Embarrassed? Or disappointed it didn't work out the way she'd hoped? I imagine a scenario where Will was meant to run off with her but chose not to for whatever reason.

"Your face was all over the news." I leave out the detail about it being discussed for half of a hot minute. "We thought you were dead, that something terrible happened to you. Where did you go?"

"I rented a car, drove up north, stayed in this little cabin in the middle of nowhere. No phone, no contact with anyone. Just me and my thoughts."

"You rented a car?" I raise an eyebrow. From what I heard, she'd left her wallet at home. "How'd you pull that off without a credit card?"

Mara's eyes flick away, just for a second, but it's enough to make my stomach tighten.

"I had help," she says vaguely.

I wait for her to elaborate, but she doesn't.

I make a mental note to check our credit card activity the second I get home.

"And Oscar?" I press. "How's he taking you being back?"

Mara shifts her weight, rubbing her arms like she's cold even though the sun is warm. "He's been overly nice. Which is . . . weird. We haven't talked about the dating app thing yet. I think we're both pretending it didn't happen."

My gaze narrows. "That's a lot to pretend away."

Her mouth twitches into a small, humorless smirk. "We've gotten pretty good at pretending over the years. It's kind of what we do best."

I don't tell her we have that in common.

"While you were gone, I talked to Oscar," I say.

Mara's eyes sharpen, but she keeps her expression neutral. "Oh?"

"He said that you weren't exactly faithful either. That surprised me given what you told me before."

Her lips press into a thin line. "Oscar says a lot of things."

Well aware.

"I don't know either of you well enough to know who to believe." I pause. "But I do know before you left, you'd been flirting with my husband."

Mara's gaze flickers, and she leans back slightly, the edge of a smirk playing at her lips. "Oh. *That's* what this is about."

"No. This is about boundaries." I keep my voice calm but firm. "I'm glad you're back and that you're safe. But from now on, you and Oscar are to stay away from my family. From Will. From me. We're neighbors, but we're not friends. We want nothing to do with . . . *this*. With your dysfunction and impulsivity. Is that understood?"

If she and Will are having an affair, if I decide to let him go and not ruin him the way I so easily could, it'll be *my* decision and on *my* timeline—not hers.

Mara blinks. If anything, she seems amused. "You think I'm a threat to your marriage?"

"I think you're a liar," I say, fueled by the fact that she isn't taking me seriously. "And you make terrible choices in life. You're weak. And quite frankly, you're not that bright either."

My cruel words roll off my tongue with frightening ease.

I could keep going, but I force myself to stop when her eyes grow glassy. If she gets emotional, she won't hear what I'm trying to say and I want to make sure she's listening, that my message is received loud and clear.

Mara studies me. "I thought we were really hitting it off, and I was looking forward to being neighbors. I'm sorry you feel this way."

We stand for a moment, the deafening quiet between us heavy with things unsaid. Then, without warning, the beginnings of her tears dry up and she shrugs, like none of this really matters to her.

"Good talk, Camille." Her tone is a blend of sarcasm and contempt, and her blue gaze now sparkles with a mix of amusement and victory before she disappears inside her house, slamming the door in my face.

As I head home, I settle onto the living room sofa and return my attention to Will's phone, and I spend the next several hours poring through every file, every photo album, every text message, every email, and every note.

The thread between him and "M" is the only damning thing I can find.

Thumb hovering over the contact card, I tap the Google number and put the call on speaker.

It rings once.

Twice.

Three times.

"Will, hi," a woman's voice answers.

But it isn't Mara.

It's a voice I'd know anywhere—one that should still be locked up in a county jail right now, not answering a cell phone.

"I thought you had class? You said you were going to call on your way home. Is everything all right?" Jacqueline asks. "Will? Are you there?"

She must be out on bail.

With my heart in my throat, I can't end the call fast enough. Hands shaking from the rush of adrenaline fueling through me, I text her from his phone—Sorry. Pocket dialed. Teaching now.

I delete the text and delete the call from the call history.

The room spins, but I anchor myself by locking my focus on a single spot—the framed wedding photo of Will and me, perched above the fireplace like some laughable emblem of trust. My fists curl at my sides, nails biting into my palms. *Jacqueline.* Of all people.

The woman who went to great lengths to ruin our marriage, to tear our perfect little family apart. The woman who tried to have me committed. The woman who implied I was an unfit mother.

While she's far from Lucinda, she's equally as deplorable.

Will and I agreed—many times—Jacqueline was no longer welcome in our lives and never would be again.

I let out a sharp exhale that does little to douse the fire spreading in my chest.

This isn't infidelity. It's worse. It's betrayal with roots that run deep—a twisted, poisonous vine strangling the trust I thought we'd built. He didn't *sleep* with her; he *violated* my trust, and that's a different kind of unforgivable.

I pace the length of the living room, my movements mechanical, my breathing shallow, thin. I'm trying not to lose control, though I'm not yet sure what I'm going to do.

All I know is I don't *do* messy. Messy is for people who aren't smart enough to channel their rage into something useful.

Something final.

Will doesn't deserve my rage.

He deserves my precision.

My next step has to be calculated—every word, every look, every move orchestrated to perfection until he won't know what hit him.

Sliding the phone onto the coffee table, I sit on the edge of the couch and close my eyes, my mind whirring as I pull threads together, crafting a plan. Jacqueline's back in his life, yes . . . but what if I'm the one who pulls her strings?

I could remind Jacqueline why I'm the last person she should underestimate.

I could remind *Will* why my trust is a currency he can't afford to spend so carelessly.

She tried to break me.

He betrayed me.

They're about to learn exactly what happens when they forget who they're dealing with.

The beginnings of a smile tug at the corners of my mouth, and it feels foreign—almost. I've always been good at fixing problems, at making inconveniences disappear.

Will's about to realize he didn't just marry someone far more dangerous than his mother ever was . . . he married Lucinda's daughter.

33

"I told Mara to stay away from us." I blurt out the words that've been on the tip of my tongue for hours. Now that I've established Mara is no longer the threat I thought she was, I'm still going to play that whole thing to my advantage. It's an easy trick—like distracting someone while you pick their pocket.

Will looks up from his laptop, one eyebrow half raised, but there's no shock in his expression. "Good."

I sit down across from him at the kitchen table, watching him carefully, waiting for him to tell me I'm making too much out of nothing. He's unnervingly calm. When he got home from work earlier, he'd asked if I'd seen his phone. I told him I accidentally grabbed his by mistake when I was leaving his office—an easy mistake seeing as how we both have the same model iPhone, both of them silver. He frowned, almost as if he doubted it, then he shrugged it off.

It took everything I had not to go ballistic on him over the Jacqueline thing, but I'm still plotting, still planning.

"You don't think I overreacted?" I bait him.

He shakes his head, shutting his computer lid with a soft click. "Not at all. Honestly, I've been thinking the same thing. Oscar's always rubbed me the wrong way."

"I thought you liked him. You were going to go golfing," I remind him.

"He invited me. I was just trying to be a good neighbor." Will leans back in his chair, arms folded, the edge of something playing on his lips. "There's just something off about him. Can't explain it. You know how sometimes you meet someone, and they seem . . . wrong? Like they're hiding something."

Hiding something—interesting choice of words.

34

"I noticed you talking to Mara a little bit ago," I say lightly as I meet Sozi at the edge of the sidewalk for our morning walk the next day, but the words come out heavier than I intended.

Sozi tucks her phone into the side pocket of her leggings.

"Yeah, she stopped me on the way over. Said she's still getting used to being home." She shakes her head. "That whole thing is insane, right? I can't imagine what was going through either of their heads during all of that . . ."

We fall into step, our strides matching as we leave Saguaro Circle. The sun peeks over the rooftops, casting long, soft shadows along the pavement. Birds chirp. The sky is a canvas of pastel blue overhead. Just another picture-perfect day in our picture-perfect neighborhood.

I only wish I could enjoy it.

"You feel sorry for her?" I ask, half expecting Sozi to scoff, but she surprises me.

"A little," she admits. "She's always been kind of lost. No idea how to deal with her emotions. And look, what Oscar did? The dating app thing? Not okay. But what she put him through wasn't any better. The two of them have got to be exhausted. They should just throw in the towel already. Put each other out of their misery."

"Couldn't agree more." I exhale sharply, already tired of the Moreno mind games.

"What does Will make of this whole thing? I saw him talking to Mara this morning," she mentions with an air of nonchalance.

My stomach plummets.

"This morning?" My voice is sharper than intended, but Sozi doesn't notice.

She's oblivious to the tension suddenly radiating off me, and I can't blame her. I've yet to tell her about my boundary-setting conversation yesterday.

While I'm no longer concerned Will and Mara are sneaking around, my request to keep our distance from the Morenos continues to fall on my husband's deaf ears—and *that's* what trips my trigger.

It's not like him to keep secrets, nor is it like him to be so obstinate. What else is he hiding? What other facets of his personality are waiting to meet me?

"Yeah, just as he was leaving for work about an hour ago. They were standing in your driveway just chatting away." She chuckles. "I didn't snap a picture this time. I thought maybe it was overkill."

Heat rises to my face, and my pulse kicks into high gear. Will *knew*. He knew I told Mara to stay away from us, from him, from our family. And yet there he was, having a friendly little chat with her, allowing her to set foot on our driveway, no less.

His mulishness sparks a blind rage in my center—sharp and painful. Will ignored my request about staying away from the Morenos, lied to me about Jacqueline, and now Mara's disregarding my crystal-clear boundaries?

These sorry souls have no idea who they're dealing with, but they're about to find out.

My hands clench into painfully tight fists at my sides, ire simmering in every part of me. As Sozi yaps on, her voice cheerful and unaware, running through neighborhood gossip and whatever drama her son's class is currently going through. I nod and mm-hmm in the right places, pretending to listen, but my thoughts are miles away.

I keep replaying the visual in my mind—Will, standing in the driveway with Mara, talking like our conversation last night never happened.

The remainder of our morning stroll passes in a blur, Sozi's voice buzzing in my ears like tuned-out background noise, my body moving on autopilot. By the time we're back to my house, I'm seething, primitive anger coiled tight like a spring.

Between this and the Lucinda letters, I'm teetering on the edge.

It's almost enough to make me snap.

35

"I brought some things. Thought we could spruce this place up a bit." I push Will's office door open with my hip, balancing a paper bag stuffed with frames from HomeGoods.

Will glances up from his desk, pleasant surprise lighting his deep blues before he smiles.

"Camille, hi." He steps around the desk and kisses me on the cheek. "Two visits in one week. How lucky am I?"

"After last time, I thought this place could use a little more personality. There's a lot going on. I feel like this room can't decide what it wants to be," I say, glancing around as if it's my creative wheels spinning and not my calculating wheels. "Plus, I needed a project. Too much time on my hands, I think."

He chuckles with amusement at his *silly little wife*, combing his fingers through his thick dark hair. The vintage watch on his wrist—one I now know to be a gift from his mother—glints in the sun that peeks in from his window.

"I won't argue—this place could use some help. But I'm about to head to class." He grabs his attaché from the chair beside me and glides the strap over his left shoulder. "You okay hanging out here for the next forty?"

"Of course." I scrunch my nose and pat his chest like the good wife that I am. "I'll get everything set up. It'll look great when you come back."

He presses a quick kiss to my temple, squeezing my arm as he heads for the door. "You're the best, you know that?"

"Don't forget it." My tone is teasing, but I'm not.

"I don't deserve you. Truly." He lingers for an extra second, drinking me in the way he does sometimes. It almost feels ordinary.

Almost.

How I wish it was.

As soon as the door clicks shut, the smile drops from my face. I place the HomeGoods bag on his desk and take a seat, shaking his mouse to wake his computer. The password prompt fills the screen. I try five of his old go-tos before I get a match, and I waste no time clicking into his work email and scrolling through the inbox. Meeting invites, student correspondence, faculty memos. Everything is tidy, professional. Will to a *T*.

Turning my attention to his folders, I go through them one by one—until I strike gold.

There's one labeled "F," containing various email chains between Will, his father George, his sister Nicola, and some attorney out of San Diego County. I can only assume the "F" stands for *family*, but at this point what does it matter?

It takes me all of ten minutes to ascertain that Jacqueline has been out on bail since we moved to Phoenix a couple of months ago, and that they're working to see if they can drop the charges and the no-contact order that Jacqueline has already violated.

Of all the things I was expecting to find today . . . this was not one of them.

My skin flushes hot, the office temperature suddenly feeling as if it could boil me alive if I don't get out of here immediately.

I take photos of all the emails using my phone, then I log off his system and leave the bag of decor untouched before getting the hell out of there. When Will asks later, I'll tell him I wasn't feeling well.

And it's the truth.

I'm feeling especially *unwell* right now.

36

"Mom, watch!" Jackson shouts, leaping off the side of the pool and cannonballing into the water. The move sends a spray of cold droplets across the patio that reaches my bare feet. Georgiana giggles, kicking her legs under the surface as she floats on a neon green pool noodle.

"That was your biggest one yet, Jack-Jack," I feign enthusiasm. Physically I'm here with my children, but my mind is elsewhere.

I lean back in my lounge chair, dabbing a towel over my legs to dry the remnants of Jackson's splash. My thoughts spin as the late-afternoon sun settles over the backyard. I check the time on my phone. As if on cue, I'm met with the familiar hum of Will's car pulling into the driveway followed by the soft thud of his door closing.

A few moments later, the back gate creaks open.

My stomach is leaden, my fists clenched, but I take a deep breath and paint a chipper expression on my face by the time he comes into view.

"Hello, hello." Will's voice is bright, overly cheerful. His casual stride and the way he's slinging his tweed jacket over his shoulder makes it look like he's coming off the best day ever.

His nonchalance only makes me detest him more. And it's a strange new reality I've been grappling with all day—resenting the man I'd have killed for up until recently.

I always loved his refreshing, simplistic honesty, how I could read this man like an open book. It was a stark contrast against the way I operated, but still—it worked for us. Or so I thought.

Will was the *one* person I trusted in this world.

That trust is gone now.

Forever.

Never to return.

He can say all the right things and give me all the foot massages and forehead kisses. He can pour me all the wine and give me all the longing, loving looks.

It's over for us.

But for now, he has no idea how short-lived his blissful unawareness is going to be.

"Sorry about the office," I say. "I wasn't feeling well. I'll come by another day and fix it up for you."

He leans down, brushing a kiss over my cheek. I don't move. As much as I want to pretend, I don't have it in me. I want to shove him as far away as I can—among many other things.

He notices I'm not receptive but says nothing, his smile faltering only slightly.

He *has* to know.

How can he not?

"Feeling better now, though?" he asks after studying me for a couple of seconds.

I nod, focusing on the kids splashing in the pool. "Just tired, I think."

Tired of his lies.

Will crouches at the edge of the pool, grinning at Georgie and Jackson. "What do you say I jump in?"

"Yes!" Jackson shouts. "Do it, Dad!"

Will glances back at me, playful, as if he thinks this'll be the thing that gets me to lighten up. "Want me to make you a drink first? I'm home. You can relax now."

"I have a headache." I stare ahead at the kids, adjusting the towel over my feet.

His gaze lingers for another moment, as if he's trying to read a foreign language between the lines.

"Okay." He claps his hand on his thigh. "Let me get changed. I'll be right back."

He disappears into the house, and the moment he's gone, I exhale slowly, trying to unclench my jaw. Being near him feels unbearable today. There's so much I want to say but can't—yet. The words sit in my throat, sharp and jagged, threatening to spill out if I open my mouth.

As soon as Will returns, swim trunks on and pool towel in tow, I head in.

I need space—from the pool, from Will, from the act I'm trying to keep up.

The house is cool, dim, and soundless—the kind of quiet that should feel like a reprieve but only makes the knot in my chest constrict harder. I stride toward the living room, intending to spend some quality time on the couch with my thoughts before I have to prepare dinner, but something out the front window catches my eye.

Mara.

She's standing outside in the cul-de-sac, her posture relaxed, her arms crossed casually over her chest. Next to her, leaning in close, is Sozi.

They're deep in conversation, heads angled toward each other, the kind of body language that implies shared secrets. Gossip. And the way they glance toward my house makes my skin prickle.

I step closer to the window, narrowing my eyes as I watch them. I can't hear them, but I'd venture to guess they're speaking in low, animated murmurs, their smiles knowing. Sozi whispers something, and Mara laughs, immediately covering her mouth as if whatever Sozi said was the kind of thing Mara had no business laughing about.

Then, as if sensing me watching, Sozi flicks her gaze toward my house again.

A few days ago this would've bothered me.

Now I couldn't care less.

Sozi and Mara are minnows.

But my husband? He's about to become shark chum.

37

"What were you and Sozi talking about just now?" I ask Will a few days later, trying my hardest to sound casual as I lean against the kitchen counter, like it's no big deal that I was just watching the two of them from inside the house.

Things between us have been bordering somewhere between lukewarm and cordial.

I'm trying to keep my cool and my distance at the same time without tipping him off. So far, I'm doing all right. He's been busy grading papers and I've been busying myself with the kids and various random household projects.

Will pauses, mid-sip from his water.

Sozi's got everyone's ear lately—except mine. She hasn't asked to go on a walk in several days. Nor has she texted me. Not that it matters. It's just not like her, is all.

"Small talk," he says, setting his glass down. "Nothing important. Never met someone who can say so much while saying so little at the same time."

I study him. "Small talk? It looked a bit more involved than that. I saw a lot of hand gestures."

"Sozi's always animated," he says. And he's not wrong. "Doesn't take much to get her excited."

"Have you talked to Mara since the other day?" I ask, glancing at him out of the corner of my eye. "I'm just wondering if she's been staying away like I asked."

Will leans back against the counter, crossing his arms loosely. "She came by earlier in the week. Asked if you were okay."

I roll my eyes. She's only pretending to care so she has an excuse to talk to Will. "Well, isn't that sweet of her."

"She said she felt horrible about making a bad impression and was worried she'd upset you." He shrugs, like it's no big deal. Nothing is ever a big deal to Will. I used to love that about him. Now it silently infuriates me. "I told her you're just protective, that's all. And that we'd prefer to keep to ourselves from now on."

I want to believe he said those exact words, but his words are officially shit now.

"How'd she take it?" I ask.

"She seemed to take it just fine." He juts his chin forward. "Said she understood. No hard feelings. Camille . . ." Will's posture straightens and his expression turns soft. He steps closer, brushing his hand over my arm. "What's going on? Seems like you've got something on your mind lately. You know you can talk to me about anything, right?"

After everything we went through in San Diego, after laying everything bare, we promised each other there would be no more secrets—ever.

I level my shoulders and stare my husband dead in the eyes. "You've been keeping secrets."

His expression stays neutral, but his complexion blanches.

"For an intelligent man," I take a step closer, narrowing the gap between us, "you've done some really, *really* stupid things."

With that, I walk away, leaving his imagination to do the rest of the work—for now.

38

The latest Lucinda letter reads like a sob story. It's almost comical at this point. I used to think her finding me would be the worst thing that could happen to my family. Now I'm beginning to think the woman isn't capable of doing anything that would land her behind bars. She's a psychological monster, not a physical one.

Not that it makes her any less harmful, but there is a difference.

> My Gabrielle—
> I know these letters are just words on a page to you, but I genuinely hope you can feel my sincerity. You're probably wondering why you're hearing from me now? After all this time? Or perhaps you're wondering how I found you. If you're feeling up to it, I'd love to tell you everything. Call me anytime—630-555-2281. Broken things can always be fixed. They might not be the same, but they can be repaired.

My thoughts are laced with indifference.

Once again, I refuse to let her take up residence in my head, not when I've got bigger fish to fry.

But for some insane reason, I program her number into my phone anyway.

39

Sozi's planted next to me at my kitchen table the next morning, her hands wrapped around the mug of coffee I handed her a minute ago. The steam curls up between us, but it does nothing to thaw the cold knot sitting in my chest.

After several days of skipping our walk—and being left out of a handful of conversations—I reached out today to invite her over. I didn't mention her inexplicable distance, nor did she bring it up. It's as if we're picking right back up where we left off. For now, I'm chalking it up to the fact that people get busy and her life doesn't revolve around mine . . . nor mine hers.

"So, what were you and Mara talking about the other day?" I ask, feigning casual amusement as I stir my latte. "Couldn't help but notice the two of you giggling like schoolgirls and glancing toward my house. Care to share?"

Sozi's brows lift, though I can't tell if she's surprised I noticed—or surprised I'm asking.

She tucks a silky dark wave behind one ear, then swallows. "You really want to know?"

I bite back my annoyance with a casual grin. "Why else would I be asking?"

"Okay. Um. We were talking about Will."

I blink, slow. "What about him?"

She leans in, as if we're coconspirators in some great secret. It's a move I've seen her do with everyone at this point. She's a bit of a whore for pot stirring and has her schtick down to a science.

"Between you and me, I'm worried Mara's obsessed with him," she says. "She told me you told her to stay away from your family. She thinks you're overreacting, but if you ask me, she was the one making a big deal about it. It's all she could talk about. And the fact that she's talking to me about it of all people . . . it clearly bothers her. And why else would it bother her?"

The air shifts. "She's the one who faked her disappearance and yet *I'm* overreacting?"

"Right? Make it make sense." Sozi gives me a sympathetic look. "She thinks Will is being more reasonable about the whole thing. Said he told her you'd calm down eventually."

The coffee in my hand feels too hot, the ceramic burning against my skin. A red haze settles behind my eyes as the words echo in my head. *Calm down eventually.*

It's one thing to suspect Mara is still indulging in her little schoolgirl crush, but it's another to hear that Will is downplaying my concerns— talking to her, reassuring *her* behind my back on top of all the other things he's been doing.

"You look upset," Sozi says, her voice soft and tinged with worry. "I shouldn't have told you."

"No, I'm fine." I sip my coffee as if it's any other day. "Just surprised my husband would say that is all."

Will was supposed to be on my side. We agreed Mara was trouble, that we'd keep our distance. And yet here he is, making me out to be the unstable one, the irrational wife who needs time to "calm down."

His behavior lately reeks of Jacqueline, the way she schemed to tip me over the edge back in San Diego, to make it seem like *I* was the irrational one when all I was trying to do was protect my children from the monster who raised me.

Is Will planning the same thing?

They say apples never fall far from the tree . . .

I nip the inside of my cheek, hard enough to taste blood.

"Honestly," she says, "I think it's good you're keeping an eye on Mara, and I hope I'm not overstepping my boundaries with any of this. Something about her doesn't sit right with me. Not since the party. And knowing her history . . . I'd just hate for her to come between you and Will."

If Mara wants him, she can have him—as soon as I'm finished.

40

"How much longer are we going to dance around this?" Will asks as he crawls into bed tonight.

I look up from my book, lashes fluttering. "Whatever do you mean?"

He takes a seat on his side, the mattress shifting with his weight, and then he exhales. "You've been distant all week—ever since you left my office. It's like you're checked out. I don't understand what's going on, Cam. I feel that you're upset with me, but I don't know why. And you won't talk to me. The other night you accused me of keeping secrets and then you walked away without explaining . . ."

"You could've asked. You chose not to."

"I'm afraid to ask you anything." His voice is raised a level. He flattens his lips, as if he's suddenly remembering the kids are asleep. "The cryptic behavior needs to stop."

I fold my book and angle myself toward him. "I couldn't agree more."

"Okay then."

We're locked in a deep stare-off for what feels like an eternity before he finally breaks.

"You go first," he says.

I chuff. "I'm not the one keeping secrets."

His mouth forms a hard line. "You and I both know that's a lie."

I lift a brow. I don't know what secrets he thinks I'm keeping, but none of them are as damning as the one he's been keeping since we moved here. Sure, I dabbled in the dating app thing for a hot minute or two, but my actions weren't an affront to our marriage or a blatant violation of our trust. I wasn't using my real name or photo. I never met anyone. It was a stupid hobby that ended just as quickly as it began.

His secret communication with his mother—a woman we currently have a protective no-contact order against, a woman we both agreed was mentally deranged and no longer a part of our family—is damning.

It's getting late.

I yawn.

The energy it's taking to fight this silent battle has been draining, and I've not come up with a solid plan—which was why I'd yet to confront him.

Plan or no plan, I can't take the pretending another minute, and the thought of spending another night asleep next to him gives me a headache. I get up, step to his side of the bed, grab his pillow, and gently shove it into his lap. Aggressive but not overly so. It's imperative I maintain some level of composure until I know how this is going to play out.

"I know your mother is out on bail and that you've been communicating with her," I say. "You should sleep in the guest room for the foreseeable future." He begins to protest, but I cut him off. "Also, I don't appreciate you telling Mara that I'd *calm down eventually*."

Will's jaw tightens, frustration flickering in his eyes.

"The cologne, the watch," I say, thinking back to the text messages from "M" that mentioned those items. "Both were gifts from your mother—not spur-of-the-moment purchases like you said. And you've been working with her attorney to drop the charges? After everything she did, after everything she put us—and our children—through . . . Need I remind you that we had to relocate our entire lives because of that woman?"

"We didn't have to—you wanted to," he says. "*You* wanted a fresh start."

I didn't want a fresh start. It was necessary.

San Diego—and our beautiful little life there—had been marred, tainted, all because of his mother.

"You think it's been easy for me? Cutting off my own mother?" he asks. "Some of us can actually feel things, you know. We're not all robots like you."

His words shoot ice through my veins, and judging by the look on his face, he realizes this a moment too late.

"Tell me what you really think of me, Will," I say, my response unaffected—or one could even argue, robotic.

Getting up from the bed, his pillow under his arm, he shuffles toward our bedroom door, stopping to turn back once he gets there. "It's late. We're tired. I shouldn't have said that. Let's revisit everything when we've had some sleep."

"I'm not sure what there is to revisit. What's done is done. You lied to me. You betrayed my trust." I fold my arms, my focus on him dagger sharp.

"I miss my mother, Camille." He exhales, pinching the bridge of his nose. When he glances over at me, his eyes are glassy, wet. If it's my sympathy he's after, he knows damn well that's something I'm incapable of giving. Even if I could, he's the last person I'd give it to right now. "She did a bad thing. Yes. But that doesn't make her a bad person. She was trying to protect her child—just like you were trying to protect yours."

"You're not a helpless six-year-old. You're a grown man. A doctor. You have a loving wife, two healthy kids, and a happy home. You can make all the excuses you want, but she didn't need to protect you."

He pauses, appearing lost in thought as he digests my words. "You're right. No. You're right. I guess this whole thing has been harder than I thought it would be. I can't just stop loving my mother. Am I angry about what she did? Yes. But she's still my mother. The thought of her in a jail cell—"

"—should be satisfying because that's exactly where people like her belong," I say. "That's where they put people who hurt others, the ones who think the law doesn't apply to them."

He groans. "I didn't tell you because I didn't want to hurt you."

"You didn't hurt me." I cock my head and give him an incredulous smile. "You *can't* hurt me. No one can. But you lost my trust. My respect, too."

His dark brows knit as worry lines spread across his forehead. "I made a mistake. I'm sorry. Surely we can fix it?"

"I'm done talking about this," I say, throat tight. "Good night, Will."

"Ridiculous," he mutters under his breath as he storms down the hall. The door to the guest room slams behind him, rattling the walls. Never mind that the children are sleeping.

I stand there, staring at the empty doorway, my heart pounding against my ribs. I should feel victorious—like I've won this argument, like I've put him in his place.

But I don't.

Instead, I feel like I've lost my footing, like I've just opened a door I can't close—I have no idea what's waiting for me on the other side.

Locking the door behind him, I make my way to bed, and before I close my eyes, I remind myself that my entire life, I've always landed on my feet—and that's not about to change now.

41

"So, when do I get to meet Ezra?" I ask the next morning. With everything that came to light about Will yesterday, home is the last place I wanted to be. Stewing and pacing won't change what he did, but clearing my head with a little distraction in the form of Sozi Hahn might keep me from going over the edge—which will prevent me from making rash decisions.

I take in Sozi's living room as I sip my coffee. She talks about him so much I feel like I know him, yet I've never seen proof of his existence. "Also, how do you keep your house so spotless with a little guy? Jackson can destroy our family room in under sixty seconds flat."

No stray toys, no colorful messes, nothing to indicate a child has ever set foot in here, let alone lives here. The couch pillows are perfectly fluffed, the books on the shelves neatly lined up, and not a single LEGO or Matchbox car in sight.

Sozi waves her hand toward a wall of built-in storage, her gold bracelets jangling.

"All his toys go in there when he's not using them. Austin hates visual clutter." She rolls her eyes. "So I make sure everything is put away before he comes home. He can't stand stuff lying around. It makes him irritable. You know those OCD types . . ."

I'd think a highly educated, modern-day woman would know the difference between "OCD" and "anal," but I bite my tongue.

I glance around the open living room and toward the kitchen, casually scanning the space for a family photo, but there are none in sight.

"Who does Ezra look like more? You or Austin?" I figure it's better than straight-up asking why she doesn't have any photos on display. She loves her kid so much she placed her career on ice to raise this child— she doesn't want to plaster his face where anyone can see it?

"Oh, you want to see pictures? We've got a gallery wall in the hallway by the bedroom. Austin doesn't like a lot of things on the walls." She rolls her eyes again. "I have to pick my battles with that man."

If I'm getting this straight, first he petitioned for her to quit her professor job to stay home and raise their kid, but he wants their home to appear as if they don't even have him—and on top of that, he won't let her hang pictures of the kid anywhere? I didn't spend much time with Austin at the party, but he seemed nice. Basic and boring, if anything. An average suburban, run-of-the-mill, middle-aged white guy.

Then again, you truly never know what people are like behind closed doors—a fact I know all too well.

Sozi leans back on the couch, crossing her legs under her.

"I promise, Ezra exists," she says with a playful grin. "I'll text you some pictures later."

"Just let me know when we can get the kids together." I sip my coffee, letting the silence settle for a beat before asking, "What's Austin been up to lately? I feel like I haven't seen him around for a minute."

She releases an exaggerated sigh, her gaze flicking to the ceiling.

"He's in Dallas for work. He's been there all week." She tosses her hair over her shoulder. "He travels a lot. Half the time, I feel like a single mom."

It makes sense why she's so desperate for attention, for interaction, why she peers out her window watching Saguaro Circle like it's her own personal reality show. She's stuck at home with a kid who's in school most of the time and a husband who travels for work. It'd be enough to make even the sanest person a little nutty.

"What about you? How are things with Will?" she asks.

The mug is suddenly too warm for my palms, so I place my coffee on a nearby coaster. I would never tell her about our fight last night. That's no one's business, especially not hers.

"Great," I say. "Same old."

"Oh, good." She smiles, but her smile doesn't reach her eyes. There's something distant in them.

"What did you say that college was that you used to teach for?" I ask.

She gives another odd smile, then chuckles. "I feel like you're grilling me today. Had I known I was going to be interviewed, I would've at least put on a suit."

"Sorry. I've just been thinking about all the walks we've taken, all the time we've spent together." I soften my delivery. "I feel like we're becoming good friends, but at the same time, I feel like I hardly know you. I don't mean to put you on the spot."

Leaning over, she brushes her hand on my knee.

"I'm messing with you. I taught at Northern Arizona. Can't wait to go back." Sozi retrieves her phone off the coffee table, a frown forming. "I'm so sorry. Ezra's school is calling. I'll be right back."

I didn't hear her phone so much as vibrate, but it could have been on silent.

"Apologies." She returns from the hallway after a minute, exasperated. "That was the preschool nurse. Apparently he's got a tummy bug—which is weird because he was completely fine this morning. Can we reschedule our little coffee date for tomorrow?"

This is entirely too convenient.

I let out a little exhale, though she doesn't notice my frustration. It's not her fault, though. My annoyance is centered on the fact that I'll have to return home now, forced to spend the rest of my day among Will's things and the life we built, which all feels like a slap in the face now that our foundation of trust and understanding has been shaken.

"Of course," I say, gathering my things. "Hope he feels better soon."

42

The following day, Sozi's house is filled with the scent of fresh citrus cleaner, the faint hum of a chic playlist you'd hear in a boutique, and meticulously arranged furniture. Lately I can't shake the sense that something isn't adding up with her.

I'm perched on her velvet sofa, legs crossed, pretending to listen as she prattles on about Ezra feeling better since yesterday. But my mind is elsewhere, as it has been these days—dizzy with thoughts circling Will, Jacqueline, Mara, and now Sozi.

She stands after a few minutes, brushing invisible crumbs off her lap as her washing machine plays a little tune from down the hall. "Back in a sec—need to switch some clothes."

As soon as she's out of sight, her phone screen lights up on the coffee table between us and a message fills the screen, bright and impossible to ignore.

MARA: Thank you so much.

Thank you for *what*?

I glance toward the hallway where Sozi disappeared, my heart thudding in my chest. I slide the phone an inch closer, just enough to confirm what I saw.

No other context—just those four words.

The sound of a humming dryer breaks my trance, and I jerk my hand back seconds before Sozi returns and settles onto the couch beside me. Her phone screen darkens before she notices the text.

"Have you talked to Mara lately?" I watch for her reaction.

"Not since the other day," she says breezily, "when she told me you were overreacting. Has she left you alone? Tell me if she hasn't and I'll say something."

"As far as I know."

It's not like Will would tell me if she were still coming around anyway.

Sozi crosses her legs, getting comfortable. "Good. I knew she'd back off eventually. She's a lot of bark and very little bite. Annoying but mostly harmless."

Harmless? That's not how Sozi's made Mara out to be. Not once. In fact, she's been insistent this entire time that Mara is essentially a threat to my marriage. Her inconsistencies are growing lazier by the day—which tells me she thinks *I'm* the idiot in this scenario.

"So you don't think I need to worry about Mara's little crush on Will anymore?" I test her.

She rolls her eyes, smirking. "Depends. How much do you trust your husband? Men are weak. Not saying Will is. Obviously you know him best. But I feel like Mara's either going to lay low for a while—or she's going to double down. I'm thinking the former. She knows you're onto her."

My patience is growing thinner by the second with this woman. "I'm sorry, but I feel like you're talking in circles with this whole Mara thing."

She blinks rapidly. "What do you mean?"

"One minute you tell me she's a husband stealer, the next minute you tell me she's harmless. Then you say it could go either way. You don't seem to like her, yet you've been talking to her quite a bit. I'm confused about where you stand."

I've learned, over the years, not to listen to people's words so much as the intention behind them. Usually you can tell what people are trying to get you to feel. Sozi's a bit different in that regard, though. It changes almost every time I talk to her—not unlike my sentiments regarding our friendship. I remind myself that, at the very least, she cures my boredom and offers me a distraction. She isn't a complete waste of time, all of the time.

Her expression hardens, her eyes squinting as she studies me. "Yeah. Okay. That's fair."

I stay silent, waiting for an elaboration that never comes.

"So . . . should I be worried?" I bait her. "Or not?"

Her mouth bunches at one side. "I'm honestly not sure. But I'll keep an eye on things. And if she says anything concerning, you'll be the first to know."

"I appreciate that," I say. "If Mara comes around my house again, if you see her and Will talking, I want you to tell me, okay?"

"I can do that. What are you going to do if you find out Will's actually having an affair?" she asks, her tone cautious but curious— almost as if she's asking out of concern, but not concern for Mara.

I smile, but it's a cold, dangerous thing. "I'm not sure."

Sozi leans back against the couch, taking me in. "You've got this. *We've* got this. It's all going to be okay . . . whatever happens."

I don't know why Sozi thinks this is a team effort, but something tells me one of these days, her watchful eyes are going to prove to be invaluable.

For that reason alone, I decide to maintain our friendship for now.

43

When I pull into the driveway that afternoon, the kids bouncing with excitement in the back seat, I spot them—Will and Oscar, standing by the edge of our yard, talking.

A flash of irritation ignites in my chest. I told Will to stay away from the Morenos, and yet here he is, blatantly ignoring me, ignoring my request.

Again.

"Inside *now*," I tell the kids, the sharp tone of my voice misdirected at them. They scramble out of the car, too distracted by their own chatter to notice the tension radiating off me. I watch them disappear through the front door before I head toward the men, each step fueled by a quiet fury.

Oscar glances my way first, a polite smile flashing briefly across his face. Will, however, doesn't look surprised. He just watches me approach with a calm, neutral expression that makes my skin crawl.

"Hi, Camille," Oscar says, giving me a nod. "I was just about to head out. Will, thanks for the talk. Camille, good seeing you."

I don't respond. I barely acknowledge him with a lightning-fast glance as he walks away, leaving just the two of us on the front lawn.

Will rubs the back of his neck and shifts his weight slightly, looking uncomfortable for the first time in a long time.

"What was that about?" My voice is cool and measured, but inside I'm burning alive, furious.

Will exhales. "He was apologizing for everything."

"Apologizing?" I repeat, skepticism dripping from the word.

"I assured him there are no hard feelings. And then I reiterated that both you *and* I would prefer to keep things cordial but distant going forward."

I narrow my eyes, searching his face for any signs of deception. The words are right—exactly what I wanted to hear—but there's something else. A flash of something darker in his eyes. He's not giving me the full story.

That or he's afraid of me, of my wrath.

And he should be.

Will takes a step closer, his expression softening.

"About the other night . . ." His voice is gentle, like he's treading carefully. "I hate fighting with you. We *never* fight. This isn't us."

He reaches out, brushing his fingers against my arm in a way that used to feel comforting. Now it just feels calculated. First he tried to play victim, justifying his choice to deceive me about Jacqueline, and now he's fawning. His actions are desperate and, at the end of the day, useless on me.

"I didn't mean to blow up," he adds. "I hate how things have been between us lately. How did we get here? How can we fix this?"

I stare at him, his words pressing against my chest like a stifling weight. This version of Will—the loving, affectionate one—isn't new. It's just not the version I trust anymore.

"You're going to have to try harder than this," I say.

Will's demeanor crumples with something that almost resembles panic. He grabs my hand, holding it tightly, like a man gripping the edge of a cliff.

"Please, Camille," he says, his voice thick with anguish. "Tell me what to do. I'll do whatever it takes to make things right again. Just tell me how to make you happy again."

I don't respond. I used to think I knew him. Will and the kids have been the closest thing I've ever known to genuine love.

Up until a month ago, I would've *died* to protect this man.

Now, he could step in front of a bus and I wouldn't try to stop him, wouldn't feel a thing.

I almost wish he were having an affair instead of talking to his mother. It's a betrayal of an entirely different variety, one I doubt anyone would understand if they weren't in my shoes. Sex is sex. My emotions are bulletproof. But my drive to protect my family? That's my Achilles' heel and Will, of all people, knows that.

The fact that he went behind my back to communicate with the evil woman who tried to destroy our happy home . . . it's unforgivable.

"I don't want to lose you," he whispers, his thumb brushing gently over my knuckles. "But I feel like I already have."

I pull my hand from his grasp, the absence of his touch cold and absolute. "I need to start dinner."

I watch the hope drain from his eyes as I turn and walk toward the house, the door clicking shut behind me with a quiet finality—the end of an era.

44

What the hell is this?

Will stands at the foot of our driveway before his night class the next evening, talking to Mara and Oscar. The three are strangely relaxed. Mara's head falls back in laughter, and Will's smile—that trademark smile of his—is easy, warm, as if nothing is wrong, as if he hasn't betrayed me by talking to them *again*.

We didn't say more than two words to one another after dinner last night, and he retired early to the guest room as soon as the kids were in bed. I spent the night plotting the logistics of how to leave him—it won't be easy given the fact that I'm financially dependent on him. It's going to take time. And a solid strategy. I'm going to have to make him think we're reconciling while I stash money away for a good attorney who can help me iron out a solid custody agreement and generous spousal support so my children won't have to suffer for their father's sins.

Should he choose to make this more difficult than it needs to be, I'll have to play dirty.

He has family money—he could afford the best attorney in the city.

But I have the kind of ruthless determination and a knack for psychological warfare that no amount of money can buy.

It's going to be a draining process, but in the end, it'll be worth it. I refuse to stay married to this pathetic liar a second longer than I have to.

I grip the frame of the front door so tightly my knuckles turn white, then I push the door open harder than necessary, the noise of it slamming against the wall cutting through the evening stillness. Will turns at the sound, his carefree expression faltering when he sees me.

Mara offers a quick wave, her gold bracelets jingling as she tucks her hair behind her ear. Oscar gives me a polite nod, though there's something guarded in his eyes. Lately it's as if the whole True Spark thing was a fever dream.

But in a near instant, the three exchange brief goodbyes and the Morenos head back toward their house.

I clearly broke up their little "party."

I stalk down the driveway, my pulse pounding in my ears.

"What was that?" I snap at Will.

Exhaustion laces his deep blue eyes. "Sozi told me about a string of break-ins down the street."

I narrow my eyes. When did he talk to Sozi? And why would she tell him before she told me? I keep my questions to myself for now.

"Break-ins?" I ask. "In a gated community?"

"Yeah, I know." He leans against the side of his car, folding his arms. "Apparently, the police think it's some teenage kid who lives around here doing it for kicks. Seems isolated to the next street over."

The weight of suspicion presses deep into my chest. "And you felt the need to relay that message to the Morenos? Personally?"

Will gifts me a calm smile, as if to overcompensate for my reaction. "I wanted to see if their security cameras have been working. Ours have been spotty lately—cutting out at weird times. Thought maybe it was an issue with our internet provider, but they said theirs are working fine. No internet issues either. Anyway, I plan on calling the security company first thing tomorrow, have someone come out and maybe replace a few. They're a little dated. Better safe than sorry."

"Since when have our security cameras not been working?"

"You haven't noticed they've been glitchy?"

I ignore his question. "How often have you been checking them? And why?"

He gives me a soft smile. "I told you, we're a team. Just doing my part to keep our family safe."

"Safe from what? From the woman you've been secretly communicating with behind my back? Make it make sense."

His smile fades, then his jaw tightens, a flicker of annoyance flashing in his eyes. "I really think you're making this into something bigger than it is."

"I don't think I am," I snap once more. "And how many times are you going to find random excuses to talk to the Morenos? After everything we've discussed? You say you want to fix our marriage—kind of seems like you're doing the opposite."

"Like it or not, the Morenos are our next-door neighbors." He shakes his head, exasperated. "We don't have to be friends with them, but we can't just act like they're invisible."

His voice is measured, but I catch the flicker of something beneath it—lingering in the space between us.

I stare, waiting for him to say more, to offer something that will make sense of this—of the cameras, the conversations, the way he continues to slip through my grasp. But he just stands before me, unruffled and composed, as if everything and everyone is perfectly reasonable—except for me.

"I'm sorry this upset you, but we need to stay safe," he says again, softer this time. "That's all I'm trying to do, Camille. Keep us safe."

I fold my arms. "Is your mother planning to pay us a visit?"

His lips part, as if he's going to say something, then thinks better of it. Shaking his head, he finally says, "No. She's not. She knows she's not welcome here."

"Then remind me, who are you protecting us from?"

His eyes hold mine for several seconds before his mouth forms a flat line.

He walks off, leaving my question unanswered.

45

"So, I talked to Mara yesterday," Sozi says the following morning, blowing gently on the surface of her coffee, her smartwatch sliding down her wrist. She's been looking a little gaunt lately. Stress?

We're standing at the edge of my driveway, the desert sun high overhead, casting long shadows across the cul-de-sac pavement the way it always does this time of day. The breeze is warm, and the air smells faintly of citrus from a tree in the Morenos' yard. We've yet to start our walk and I'm not sure we will at this point. Her sneakers seem firmly planted.

"Oh, yeah?" I'm all ears, though every word she says feels like another thread in the knot pulling tighter inside me. "What'd she have to say?"

Sozi glances toward the Morenos' house, her eyes lingering there a little too long. "She couldn't stop talking about how lucky you are to have Will. Kept going on and on about it."

My heart skips. "Lucky?"

Sozi nods, her gaze still pinned to Mara's house.

"Yeah. That's the word she used. She said you and Will seem really happy." She pauses, turning toward me, a knowing smirk tugging at the corner of her mouth. "I think she's projecting. She seems miserable with Oscar, even after everything."

The last several times I've seen the Morenos together, they seemed fine. It could be an act. But there've not been any signs of distress on either of their faces. No sounds of breaking glass. No one crying on the front steps.

I follow her gaze to the front of the Morenos' house, the perfect stucco exterior hiding whatever rot may or may not lie beneath. "Miserable how?"

Sozi shrugs. "Well, they've obviously been having marital issues, and I think it's easy to assume other couples are happier than we are, especially when we're in that kind of place. I told her that, too. I said she shouldn't assume you and Will are any happier than anyone else."

I arch a brow. "You told her that?"

She gives me a sly grin. "Not in so many words, but yeah. I told her to let it go. It's not a good look, and fixating on other people's marriages is not doing her any favors, especially if she wants to fix her own. And I think she does. Though Will's been a bit of a distraction for her. A fantasy, I think. Ever heard of limerence? She's got it bad—for your husband, I'm afraid."

I've read about limerence. It can be powerful, all-consuming, making people act in ways they wouldn't normally. It's a crush on steroids. But I can't shake the feeling that it's Sozi doing the projecting—what if she's the one pining over Will, not Mara?

"How's Ezra doing? You realize we still haven't gotten the kids together." I let the statement hang in the air. I get that people are busy, kids especially, but as much time as I've spent with this woman and as much as she's talked about him—combined with the lack of evidence of his existence—I'm having serious doubt the child exists.

Sozi doesn't miss a beat. "He's great. Austin took him to his grandparents for the weekend to stay with them for a few days. They've got a condo in Sedona. He loves it up there—the windy drive, the mountains. It's his favorite place."

I nod slowly, trying to fit the pieces together in my mind. "Send me a picture of him sometime. I'd love to get Jack and Georgie excited about meeting him when he gets back. There aren't a lot of kids on our street."

"Of course," Sozi says with a bright smile, but once again the look doesn't quite reach her eyes. She glances down at her phone, but I hadn't heard it buzz. And once again, her interruptions have convenient timing. "Ah. I'm so sorry. Austin's calling. I should take this."

She gives me a quick wave, her voice already shifting into polite professionalism as she answers the call. "Hey, is everything okay? Hang on. Give me one sec."

I watch her disappear into her house, her dark ponytail swaying behind her. I linger in the sun, rooted in place, my mind spinning. Something isn't adding up.

I finally think I have an idea why.

Later that night, after the kids are asleep and Will is busy in the other room, I curl up on the couch with my laptop and type "Sozi Hahn" into the search bar on a popular social media site.

A couple of profiles pop up. None with photos of Ezra. None with mentions of Austin. No family posts. Nothing about a husband or a child. No hint of Hahn being a married or maiden name.

I search deeper, clicking through tagged photos and old posts. It's tedious, slow work, but then—finally—I find it.

A Facebook group photo from a family reunion in 2019, posted by someone I can only assume is a relative of hers. The caption reads: **Hahn Family Reunion—Boston! So glad to see so many familiar faces!** I zoom in on the photo, which is three rows of people deep, until I pick out Sozi smiling stiffly beside an older woman who looks vaguely like her.

The comments tell a different story.

BRENDA SCHOONOVER: How's Sozi doing these days? Haven't heard from her in forever.

ROB HAHN: Last I heard, she moved out west—
Arizona or New Mexico, I think. Hope she's doing okay.

Another comment catches my eye, and it sends a chill down my spine.

STASI HAHN: Honestly, I hope she stays there.
I think she's burned every bridge there is on the east
coast.
BRENDA SCHOONOVER: Come on, be nice,
@Stasi. That's your sister.
STASI HAHN: Not by choice @Brenda.
KARA SCHOONOVER: Sozi seemed to be doing
better at the reunion . . . I'd hoped she was on a better
path.
STASI HAHN: She must've had you fooled, @Kara.
She's pretty good at that. Last I heard she was on "hus-
band" number six and has somewhere between zero and
four children, depending on who you ask.

I sit back, staring at the screen, my pulse racing.
There are no other photos of Sozi.
Just a laundry list of estranged relatives and unanswered questions.

46

I scrape the last bit of pasta from the plates into the trash the next evening, the sound of silverware clinking against porcelain filling the quiet kitchen. I didn't walk with Sozi today. I couldn't. Not after everything I found last night—her estranged family, the gray area about Austin and Ezra. And to top it off, she still hasn't sent me a single picture of that so-called son of hers.

It shouldn't bother me as much as it does, especially when I have bigger fish to fry. I suppose my therapist would tell me Sozi is "triggering." The lies and manipulation, the lengths she went to to craft this facade of a phony life, it all reeks of Lucinda.

The annoyance in my chest tightens as I rinse the plates and load them into the dishwasher. I keep running through it all in my head: the fake husband, the invisible child, the way Sozi has casually yet persistently concerned herself with my marriage while using Mara to divert suspicions.

It's crystal clear . . . now.

When the last dish is in, I wipe down the counter and sweep my hair out of my face, trying to shake off the agitation that clings to me like a second skin these days. Tying up the half-full kitchen trash, I haul it to the bin by the garage to get some fresh air.

That's when I see it.

An empty bottle of Mara's favorite rosé sitting at the top of the trash bin.

I didn't open any wine tonight—or last night, for that matter.

I push aside a crumpled paper towel and find something else: a torn-up thank-you note scattered among various food wrappers and trash bags. My heart skips as I pluck the pieces out, assembling them carefully on the pavement.

Will—
Thank you so much. You always know exactly what I need.
—M

I stand there for a moment, staring at the bottle and the note, my icy pulse quickening with every shallow breath. This whole thing reeks of Sozi, but I've got the overwhelming urge to confront Will anyway—to test his reaction.

I grab everything and march back inside, where Will is sitting on the couch, scrolling through his phone.

"Hey." My voice is sharp, cutting through the quiet hum of the TV. I hold up the note and the bottle. "Care to explain this?"

Will looks up, confused. "What is that?"

"I found it in the trash. An empty bottle of Mara's favorite wine and a thank-you note. From *M*." I narrow my eyes, searching his face for any flicker of guilt or recognition.

He stares at it for a moment, then slowly shakes his head. "It was sitting by my car when I went to leave for work this morning."

I blink, not buying it. Someone clearly planted this. Whether it was Will, Mara, or Sozi remains to be determined.

"It was just . . . there," he says, his voice low, calm but edged with discomfort. "The bottle and the note. I didn't know what to make of it, so I dumped it out in the yard, ripped up the note, and tossed it all."

"And you didn't think to tell me?" I ask. "You just threw it away like it was nothing?"

Will scrubs a hand down his face. "I'm just as freaked out as you are. I swear I didn't know what to do with it. I was in a hurry, running late for work. I completely forgot about it until now."

I press my lips into a thin line, trying to control the rage simmering just beneath the surface. "Did you check the cameras?"

Will nods.

"I already looked." He pulls out his phone, taps the screen, and hands it to me. "All we got is this."

I press play on the footage. At 3:04 AM, a shadowy figure appears at the edge of the frame, their features impossible to make out. Their frame is on the petite side—similar to both Sozi and Mara. They're dressed entirely in black, moving quietly and deliberately as they set something down by the garage door. The figure glances around, their face hidden beneath a hood, and then slips out of view.

There's no way to tell where they came from—or where they went.

"Told you our cameras have been acting up lately. The security company said the soonest they could send someone out is next Friday," he says.

I hand the phone back to Will, my pulse hammering in my ears. "That doesn't tell us much."

Only that it was a setup.

But who set it up?

"No, it doesn't," Will agrees, leaning back with a sigh. "But I swear to you, Camille, on my life—Mara has no reason to leave me wine or thank me for anything. I barely know her."

"Sozi . . ." I don't finish my thought.

Will looks at me, his brow furrowed. "What about her?"

"Things aren't adding up," I say, crossing my arms. "I looked her up last night. There's no mention of a husband named Austin or a son named Ezra. None of it. And her family? They're estranged. They haven't heard from her in years."

Will stares at me, processing.

"Sozi's always seemed a little . . . off," he admits. "But I thought you two were friends, and I was glad you were making friends so I never said anything."

I think of the comments her relatives made, about her fooling people, about her obsession with Mara's obsession with Will. It's exactly the kind of master manipulation Lucinda would've done.

I hate that I underestimated her, that she insulted my intelligence. I, of all people, should've seen through it with X-ray vision precision. It's infuriating.

She's lucky I'm a woman with too much to lose.

"You think Sozi did that?" Will scratches at his brow, seeming genuinely perplexed.

This time *I* walk away, leaving his question unanswered.

I don't think Sozi's behind this—I know she is.

47

Mara's standing on the front lawn the next afternoon, watering the small patch of jasmine flowers near her porch. She glances up when she sees me walking toward her, her expression flat and unwelcoming when she does a double-take. The chill in the air between us is unmistakable.

"Can I help you, Camille?" she asks, voice steeped in annoyance.

I stop just a few feet away, not daring to get too close. "I need to talk to you. In confidence."

Mara lets out a small, humorless laugh. "What now? Another demand? Another accusation?"

"I just want the truth." I look her in the eye. "Are you in love with my husband?"

Mara stares at me, stunned for a moment, then scoffs. "God, no. Where is this even coming from?"

I hold out the ripped thank-you note. "To be fair, you have an extensive history of lying."

And that's what this is about. She's nothing but an obnoxious liar. A nuisance. A sad, desperate, broken woman, and I've got more important issues demanding my attention. This whole issue needs to be put to bed, and that's exactly what I'm here to do.

"That's not even my handwriting," she says. "And why would I thank Will for something? What did he do for me exactly?"

"Sozi said—"

Mara cuts me off instantly, her eyes flashing wild. "*Sozi?* Did Sozi give you this impression?"

I pause, thrown by the sudden venom in her tone.

Mara lets out a bitter laugh, crossing her arms. "Let me give you some advice that's the God's honest truth: Sozi is the last person you should trust."

"What do you mean?"

Mara looks down, rubbing her temple as if exhausted by the whole conversation. "I feel stupid even admitting this, but . . . she's what I'd call a master manipulator. She actually helped me disappear that week. It was her idea. She orchestrated the whole thing."

My heart skips a beat. "What?"

"I was in a bad place. You know that. You saw it firsthand—along with the rest of Saguaro Circle," Mara says, shame lacing her words. "Sozi insisted I'd feel better taking a breather from everything, that it would help Oscar and me to calm down and think rationally so we could fix our marriage. Said she could set me up in a cabin in Sedona. Gave me a burner phone for emergencies. Rented me a car. She took care of everything. If I'd have used my credit card, he'd have tracked me down and then we wouldn't have had the space I thought we needed at the time. I regret it all now, of course."

"Do you?" I ask, my throat tight.

"Of course. It only made things worse." Mara appears genuinely remorseful, but then again, it doesn't take much for her to emote anything. "It was reckless. I could've gotten arrested. And it was awful to put Oscar through something like that. He truly thought I was dead. He was beside himself. I wasn't thinking clearly, and I'm so embarrassed. Worst of all? She promised she'd assure him I was okay, that she knew where I was and when I was returning . . . and she didn't. She let him think something happened to me. That wasn't the plan."

She was pretty upset before she left. It's easy to take advantage of someone in that state, especially if you're good at that kind of thing.

"He only went on that stupid dating app because of what *I* did. I cheated on him once. A couple months ago with a tennis pro at the clubhouse. Talk about cliché." She looks away, wincing as if the shame of uttering those words physically hurts. "Biggest mistake of my life. That's why I denied it to you. I didn't want to rehash it, and sometimes it's easier to pretend it didn't happen, even though Oscar won't let it go."

She glances back at me, her expression softening.

"We've *both* made mistakes. I won't pretend we're perfect. We're far from it. But I deeply regret if anything I did made you feel uncomfortable or made you feel like your family wasn't safe around us."

For the first time, there's a flicker of sincerity in her voice, and against my better judgment, I soften a little.

I *want* to believe her.

But giving people the benefit of the doubt has proven to be the last thing I should be doing around here.

We're nothing but a circle of strangers.

I fold my arms, shifting my weight. "What were you and Will talking about the other day? He mentioned the break-ins."

Mara's brow furrows. "Break-ins? What break-ins?"

My pulse quickens.

Mara seems genuinely clueless. "He was asking about Sozi and Austin. Oscar and I thought it was weird—he wanted to know how long they'd been together, when I last saw Austin, stuff like that."

Interesting he was asking the Morenos about Sozi and Austin before I'd brought up my concerns about Sozi. How—and why—was he ahead of that curve?

I frown. "Why would he ask that?"

Mara shrugs. "Probably because they broke up? At least I think they have because I haven't seen him around in a while. They weren't married. Ezra was Austin's kid from a previous relationship. They only had him part-time. They weren't even together for more than a couple of months. All of her relationships, if you can call it that, tend to crash and burn, over as quickly as they began. I think they bounce once they realize she's not exactly stable. My theory anyway."

I blink, trying to piece it together. After what I've gleaned about Sozi, I believe Mara. Still, the gravity of her words crashes over me because Will lied to me again. He made up the story about the break-ins. The question now is: *Why?*

Mara glances at the time on her phone. "I'd love to keep talking, but I've got to run. Got a hair appointment in the valley and I need to get going to get ahead of traffic. Can we pick this up later?"

I nod, mind racing. "I have to pick up the kids from school anyway."

Just as I turn toward my car, my phone buzzes in my pocket. I pull it out and see a text from Sozi. If I know her at all, she had to have been watching us talking.

SOZI: Can we talk?

I exhale sharply, my jaw clenching.

I fire off a response.

ME: I don't think that's a good idea.

Three dots appear, then vanish, then appear again. Finally, her response comes through.

SOZI: ???

SOZI: I'm confused . . . is everything okay?

My blood runs cold. I hit call instead of texting back, needing to hear her voice for this.

She answers on the first ring. "Camille, hey—"

"Listen," I cut her off, keeping my voice steady but firm. "You are the *worst* kind of person. I want nothing to do with you from here on out."

She's quiet on the other end, the silence stretching thick and heavy between us.

"Where is this coming from?" Her voice is laced with confusion, but whether or not it's genuine is impossible to tell. "Camille, I don't understand . . . did you talk to Mara? What did she say?"

The fact that she instantly blames Mara tells me everything I need to know.

"I'm done with you," I reiterate, my voice low. "Don't come near me or my family again. Don't call me. Don't text me. Don't watch me. Don't so much as breathe in our direction. If you do, I'll make damn sure you wish you didn't."

There's a sharp intake of breath on the other end, like she's about to respond, but I don't give her the chance. I end the call and immediately type out a follow-up text.

ME: So we're clear and so this is in writing: don't come near me or my family again. Don't call. Don't text. Don't so much as breathe in our direction. You're dead to us.

I hit send on my cruel but necessary text and stare at the screen, waiting for those three dots to appear again, certain she'll protest.

But she doesn't.

Satisfaction marinates in my bones.

I'll throw her away like the trash she is, and I won't think about her again.

She's a pest, a nuisance, and once starved of the attention she so desperately seeks, and like all pests, she'll buzz off if she wants to survive.

48

I pull into the garage after school pickup, the steady drone of my engine cutting out as I press the start/stop button. The kids are in the back seat, bickering about which cartoon we'll put on when we get inside, but I'm too exhausted to care. It's Will's late night, too. He's been at school all day and he'll be teaching a night class. I'll be lucky if he rolls in before 10:00 PM.

My head is buzzing, a constant low thrum of stress that hasn't left me since my most recent conversation with Sozi.

That's when I see it.

Something dark in the corner of the garage, in the third stall, the one we use for bicycles and wagons and the various yard toys we've accumulated over the years.

I squint, attempting to make out the shape, but it's just out of the light's reach. Whatever it is, it doesn't belong here. It wasn't here when I left a couple of hours ago.

"Come on, guys," I say, forcing my voice to stay light. "Let's get inside."

Jackson and Georgie scramble out of the car, still squabbling, oblivious to the weight settling over me and the cool sweat collecting over my brow. I usher them inside as quickly as possible, locking the door behind us with an almost frantic twist of my wrist.

"How about some Disney Channel and chocolate chip cookies?" I offer a cheerful distraction. I rarely give them cookies as an after-school snack, but neither of them dare question it.

The two of them perk up almost instantly, their earlier argument forgotten, and I set them up in front of the TV with a bowl of Chips Ahoy! I hid for myself in the back of the pantry a few weeks ago. Within seconds, the bright colors of the cartoon flicker across their faces, and their little eyes are glued to the screen.

I linger long enough to ensure they're captivated by the TV before slipping back through the door into the garage. The cold cement floor sends a chill up my legs as I flip on the overhead light. The bulb hums to life, casting harsh, artificial light across everything.

Approaching the corner with slow, careful movements, my heart hammers in my throat.

And then I see her.

Sozi.

Her lifeless body lies crumpled against the floor near the corner, her dark hair slicked with blood, her bronzed face an abnormal shade of pale. Her white top is soaked with crimson and her jeans are stained with uneven patches of blood—there are so many stab wounds I can't begin to count them. Beside her rests a butcher knife, the blade stained with dried smears of black-red gore.

A metallic scent fills my nostrils, sharp and nauseating.

Frozen, I study the mess of Sozi's remains, waiting for some kind of reaction to wash over me.

Shock. Panic. Grief. Horror.

Anything.

Nothing comes.

My mind whirs instead, a thousand thoughts firing all at once, dizzy with possible scenarios and motives involving Mara and Sozi, but none of them quite add up . . . except for one.

Perhaps Sozi was telling the truth all along and Mara wanted to silence her—and frame me—to clear the path for her to have Will. Sozi's easy prey, too—estranged from her family. No one will miss her. If she and Austin are broken up, he won't report her missing.

But if he does . . .

I think about my last text to her, the one where I told her to stay away, the one where I threatened her. If that was our final exchange and she's found dead in my garage, I'll be an immediate person of interest.

I fumble with my phone, pulling up the security camera app. My fingers tremble so badly I almost drop it. When the app loads, my heart sinks.

The exterior cameras are all offline.

Apparently Will wasn't lying when he said the system was acting strange lately.

There's no footage; no way to prove who came or went, no record of who's responsible for the dead body in my garage.

I close my eyes, trying to think clearly amid a haze of dizzying thoughts. If I can just get the kids to bed, I can clean this up—at least enough to get through the night. Enough to buy me some time to figure out the next step. Whoever did this to Sozi left her here for *me* to clean up.

And if I don't, it's all over for us.

But in cleaning her up, I risk incriminating myself if I leave evidence behind.

I don't have a choice.

I can't do anything about this until the kids are asleep, which will be several hours from now—enough time for me to think this through. Returning inside, I tend to the children, make dinner, and run baths like it's any other night, all the while strategizing in silence.

Four of the longest hours of my life pass before I finally return to the garage.

Except it's the strangest thing . . .

There's no metallic tang of blood hitting me like a wall.

No trace of early decay lingering in the air.

No lifeless, human-shaped lump in the northwest corner of the third stall.

With my heart inching up my throat, I smack the nearby light switch, missing it on the first attempt. The lone overhead light buzzes to life, casting a sterile glow over spotless concrete.

The butcher knife is gone.

The blood is gone.

And so is Sozi's body.

49

The door clicks shut softly, and I listen to Will's familiar footsteps as he moves through our house, dropping his keys on the console table by the door, shrugging off his jacket and hanging it in the hall coat closet, opening and closing the fridge, shuffling around.

The kids are asleep. The house is dark. I'm lying perfectly still in our bed, pretending to be out cold despite the fact that my mind is racing—caught in a relentless loop of what-ifs and worst-case scenarios.

It hasn't stopped all night. Not once.

In fact, it's only grown more intense in the two hours that have passed since the dead body went missing.

Will's footsteps grow louder as he approaches the bedroom, stopping outside the door. Peeking through slitted eyes, I spot the shadows of his feet at the bottom of the door. He's been sleeping in the guest room since our big fight and I expect him to do the same tonight, which is why it's concerning that he's standing in the hall outside our bedroom, lingering.

The soft creak of our door hinges sends my heart lurching to my throat.

A moment later, the bed shifts as he sits on the edge.

He's quiet for the longest moment, and I can almost feel him watching me, the heat of his gaze heavy on my face.

"You're not asleep." He breaks the silence. His voice is low, steady, but most of all, knowing. "I just saw you swallow."

He leans closer, brushing a hand lightly down my arm.

"Talk to me," he whispers, his breath warm against the back of my neck, though it's more commanding than endearing.

Does he know?

"Camille, enough of this." His hand grips my arm, and he gives me a good shake, enough to wake me up had I been truly out cold.

I open my eyes, meeting his in the dark. His shape is illuminated by the hallway light spilling in from the doorway.

My mind circles back to Mara, like it has been all night. If she and Will were somehow in this together, maybe the disappearance thing was to frame Oscar but it backfired? Maybe Sozi wasn't in on it, but Mara blamed her because given her history of lying, it wouldn't be hard for anyone to believe? Maybe Sozi was being honest the whole time about Mara's obsession—and about trying to tell Mara to leave Will alone.

Maybe Mara killed Sozi as a way to shut her up and frame me at the same time.

If I go down, Will would be free—a single man.

My husband exhales, dragging his hand through his thick dark hair as his shoulders fall.

What if Will and Mara orchestrated this entire thing? Mara is stunning and wasted no time flirting with my husband the second she laid eyes on him. I used to put the man on a pedestal, but after everything that's come to light lately, I now know he's not who I thought he was.

Not even close.

The mattress dips slightly as Will shifts. Then, with a click, the soft glow of the bedside lamp flickers to life. I wince, my eyes adjusting to the light.

"Camille," he says. "I need you to look at me because we're going to have a talk. A very important talk. And we're having it right now."

His blue eyes are stormy, laced with determination.

The thought of Will orchestrating this whole thing with Mara turns my entire thought process upside down. He *couldn't*. He was at work all day and taught class all evening. He wouldn't have had time to murder Sozi, then come home and clean it up while I was inside making dinner. The whole thing is absurd enough without twisting it into something implausible.

His hand moves to mine, squeezing gently. "It's going to be okay."

He knows.

He has to.

But technically, he doesn't know that I know. I could play dumb—he doesn't know I noticed the body in the corner of the garage, which means I wouldn't know anything about it being cleaned up and removed while I was inside with the kids.

His hand tightens on mine, his expression hardening.

"Come with me," he says, his voice low and uncompromising.

Wrapping his hand around my wrist, he pulls me until I'm sitting up, then he peels the covers off me and tosses them aside with one fluid movement.

"Where?" I ask.

He rises off the bed, my wrist still in his firm grip. "Just come with me."

50

The air outside is cool and heavy, carrying the faint scent of night-blooming jasmine from the Morenos' yard. Will and I step out onto the patio, each holding a drink. Bourbon on the rocks for him, double vodka for me.

I'm sticking to my script of playing dumb and so far, it seems to be working. For all intents and purposes, Will thinks I'm tired, half asleep, unaware that anything's amiss other than the state of our marriage, and simply annoyed that he's making us talk at this ungodly hour.

I settle into one of the wrought-iron chairs, cradling my glass, but Will remains upright, swirling his drink in his hand as if the motion will calm him.

It doesn't.

He's a live wire—tense, pacing back and forth under the eerie light of a full moon.

"We have a serious problem," he finally speaks. "And we have to fix it. *Together.*"

I can think of a whole slew of serious problems we're facing at the moment.

Coolly, I take a slow sip of my drink, keeping my face carefully neutral. "Can you be more specific?"

Will stops pacing, turning to look at me. His eyes glint in the soft moonlight, filled with something intense yet desperate at the same time.

"There's nothing you can say or do that'll change how I feel about you. You know that, right? *Nothing.*" He takes a step closer. "I've been obsessed with you since the moment I saw you in that pub in Chicago—O'Horan's, the one just outside the hospital. Do you remember?"

I nod, though my throat tightens at the memory of the night we first met.

"You were so classy," he continues, his voice soft and nostalgic. "Enigmatic. Poised. And you had this look in your eyes, like you knew more than you were letting on. That you had depth. That you could challenge me in ways I needed to be challenged. I knew right then—I had to have you. There was a moment that night, when you looked over at me, and I melted. All I kept thinking was . . . how can I have this for the rest of my life?"

Will has never shared this with me. Now I can't help but wonder why.

He paces more, stopping once to take a generous swig of bourbon. "When we started dating, you were *perfect*, like you were made just for me."

I stare into my glass.

"That was intentional," I say, voice flat. "That's what I do, Will. I manipulated you into thinking I was perfect for you. And it worked."

"Regardless, you *chose* me." His eyes are wild in a frightening way. "You *wanted* me. You wanted this life, this family. And I wanted you, so I gave it all to you. This beautiful life. I gave you *everything* you wanted."

"You did."

"So why," he whispers, the words raw with frustration, "are you throwing it all away? Like it's nothing? Like it never mattered at all?"

I look up at him, meeting his gaze head-on. "I should be asking you that question."

Will's jaw tightens, and his hand trembles slightly as he raises the glass to his lips. He takes a long drink, then exhales through his nostrils. "I know about you and Oscar."

I freeze. "What?"

"I found the True Spark app on your phone several weeks ago, Camille. I went through the messages. You and Oscar had been talking, you even met up at some coffee shop. I followed you there. I saw the two of you go inside. Then you deleted the app after that. You buried the evidence. You took it offline." His words come out faster with each sentence, like the man's unraveling in real time. "I thought I was doing everything right to make you happy. But *Oscar*? Of all people?"

The ground beneath me shifts, though my whole world might as well be tilting off its axis.

"It's not what you think," I say. "Not at all."

Will chuffs. "I want to believe you. God, I want to. But you said so yourself—you manipulate people. It's what you do. I can't believe anything you say. You know that. All I know is what I saw."

He drops into one of the patio chairs, crumpling like a man who's carried too much for too long.

Deafening quietude branches between us, thick and stifling in spite of the dry air that surrounds us, filled with everything we aren't saying—like the dead body that was lying in our garage earlier tonight.

Will scrubs his hands over his face, exhausted.

"You can't leave me, Camille. Not after everything we've built together. Not after everything we've been through. You can't do that to the kids. To me." His voice cracks at the edges. "I can't lose you. I don't know who I am without . . . us."

Will's words are laced with emotion and his eyes turn wet. The number of times I've seen this man in this state over the course of our marriage, I could count on one hand. He's always been composed, collected, confident.

"Neither of us is perfect." Taking a seat, he reaches across the table toward me, but I don't extend my hand to his. "But together, *we're* perfect."

I straighten my shoulders and keep my composure as I collect my thoughts. I thought he wanted to talk about the dead body in the garage. I wasn't ready for *this* conversation.

Clearing my throat, I tell him, "I wasn't planning on leaving, nor was I planning to meet Oscar. If you took the time to—"

"—that's not what Sozi said." He interrupts me before I can explain that if he'd have looked at my actual profile, he'd have seen the AI avatar.

But his mention of Sozi hits me like a slap.

"When were you talking to Sozi?" I ask.

He sighs, resting the side of his face against his hand. "This afternoon. I had to run home and grab something from the house before my evening class, and she stopped over, said she was looking for you."

Oh, God.

On the outside, I remain calm. Inside, I'm certain I know where this is going. "What else did she say?"

Will shakes his head, staring into our darkened yard. "She said she was concerned about you—said you've been acting erratically, paranoid. Obsessing over Mara . . . worried I was cheating . . ."

He glances back, his eyes lingering on mine. "She told me you drink all day. That the kids are left outside alone all the time."

The ice in my vodka cracks against the glass. "What was she getting at?"

"She didn't think you were a good mother. Or a good wife." Will's voice tightens. "She said you didn't deserve me."

The air between us is more charged than ever, and I watch him carefully, waiting for the next shoe to drop, holding my breath until I know where he's going with all of this.

"But I told her none of that was true." He takes another careful sip, finishing the rest of his liquor before placing his tumbler on the table and leaning back.

Was it Will?

Did *Will* kill Sozi?

My husband leans forward, his chin tucked. "Then I told her to leave."

"And?" My voice is barely a whisper.

"And she didn't like that very much." His lips press flat. I stay silent, waiting for him to continue. Only now his eyes are hollow and unfamiliar, those of a total stranger. "But the thing is, Camille, it wasn't the first time she'd come over to talk to me. Wasn't even the second. But it was the first time she told me she was falling in love with me, that I deserved better than you, that the kids deserved better than you. She said if I didn't give her a chance—if I didn't want her—she'd make me regret it. She'd accuse me of something awful. She'd do everything she could to destroy us."

A sick, heavy silence falls over us. My heart pounds painfully in my chest as I stare at the man sitting across from me.

"She hardly kn—*knows*—you." I catch myself before I used the wrong tense. We've yet to establish I know Sozi's dead.

Sozi might have been a lot of things, but declaring her love for someone she hardly knew? Even Lucinda didn't do that. She'd have played a longer game, not come off blatantly psychotic.

"That bottle of wine and the thank you note from 'M'?" Will says. "That was Sozi. I suspected it then, but I didn't have proof. She also admitted to working hard to make you think Mara was obsessed with me. I kept wondering why you were so fixated on that, Camille . . . it made no sense. Sure she flirted with me at a party, but other than a few conversations in the driveway and having them over a couple of times, she was only ever neighborly."

Framing those interactions through a new lens, Will is right.

But it doesn't necessarily mean he's being honest.

If Mara and Will were in on this together, this would be the perfect way to make Sozi out to be the bad guy, to take the heat off them.

"Why do you think I was so concerned about the security cameras?" he asks. "I knew she was coming around here, doing God knows what."

"Why didn't you tell me? You knew we were friends. This makes no sense."

"I didn't realize how unhinged she was. I thought it was an innocent crush at first—and honestly, I was more upset about you and Oscar."

I want to interject about the Oscar thing again, but he's intent in this moment, shedding light on the Sozi thing, and I don't want to jump to a topic that's—at this point—moot.

"Sozi refused to leave, she kept threatening our marriage, our happiness, everything we've worked so hard for. I did what I had to do to protect us.

To keep our family safe." He looks at me, and in that moment, I don't recognize him. "You've been protecting us for so long. It was my turn."

"What are you saying?"

He swallows hard, his jaw clenched, like a man who's about to confess a carnal sin.

"I didn't want to." His voice is a strained whisper. "I had to."

"You had to *what*?"

Will doesn't move, doesn't speak. His utter silence and the knowing stare he gives me is louder than any confession.

I can't believe he did this to us.

I can't believe he'd be so stupid to invite this kind of stress and conflict into our lives—and for *what*?

This could've been a conversation—not a goddamn murder.

I rise, fuming, but before I can get too far, he grabs me by the wrist, pulling me back toward him with a grip that's almost painful.

"You can't go to the police," he says. "You can't tell *anyone*."

He holds me there, his eyes pleading and commanding all at once. But beneath the desperation, I see something else, something I've never seen in this man before.

Control.

"If you go to the police," Will draws his words out with careful precision, "I'll make sure you're implicated, too. We're in this together, Camille. If I go down, you go down with me." He pauses, as if to give me time to process his threat. "And if you *don't* go down with me, I'll make sure the kids go to my sister in Germany . . . or my father. Not you. I think we both know that's a realistic possibility given your history. All I'd have to tell them is . . ."

The words loom, menacing me in the night air. He doesn't need to finish his warning. We both know how ugly this could get.

I study my stranger of a husband in an entirely different light. This isn't the man I married. The man I married saves lives, he doesn't take them, doesn't ruin them.

This is someone else entirely—Jacqueline and Lucinda combined.

While I'm furious at this revelation, I'd be lying if I said I wasn't also impressed . . . because if things were reversed, I'd have handled it the same way.

But I'm . . . *me*.

And Will is . . . not.

I've always held him to a completely different set of standards, standards that allowed me to respect and trust him.

All of it means nothing now.

I take a slow, deliberate breath, forcing a mask of unbothered-ness over my face. I've dealt with both of those women before and come out on top. I'll deal with Will, too.

"Will," I say, blinking and feigning shock before softening my expression into something akin to deep appreciation. Even if he knows my emotions are fake, it's difficult for the average person not to believe what they desperately want to believe—and Will desperately wants to believe he singlehandedly saved our marriage and found a way to keep me from running into the arms of someone else.

I reach across the table, offering my hand. He interlaces our fingers, trapping mine tight between his.

"You did what you had to do," I continue. "Just like I would have. I can't tell you how much that means to me. How much it impresses me. This kind of thing, it'd be easy for *me* to do. But not you. You risked a lot and you risked it for our family."

His hold loosens. "I knew you'd see it my way."

Rising from his seat, he moves to me, pulling me up and wrapping me so close against his chest I can feel his heart hammering. He's exhilarated. Relieved. Stupid.

He kisses me hard, and like the good wife he still so badly wants me to be, I kiss him back.

Will doesn't feel it, but my heart is colder than ice.

And he doesn't know it yet, but this kiss has officially sealed his fate.

51

The checkout line is moving fast as I load the last of my groceries onto the conveyor belt—just a few things to get us through the next couple of days. Bananas for Georgie's lunchbox, alphabet cereal for Jackson, and a few ingredients for tonight's dinner—chicken cordon bleu. It's Will's favorite and I haven't made it in a while. It's also a strategic move, one to help him believe he has nothing to worry about with me, that I'm grateful for what he did.

"That'll be $43.76," the cashier says, still smiling.

Declined.

The word flashes on the screen, bright and unforgiving. The man in line behind me rises on the balls of his feet, his caterpillar brows lifting as he silently judges me.

"Well, this is strange." I force a tight smile. "Let me try that again."

I swipe the card a second time, slower, holding my breath.

Declined.

I pull another card from my wallet, hands trembling now, and try again.

Declined.

The cashier's friendly smile weakens. She glances toward the growing line behind me, her polite demeanor moments from slipping into impatience. "Want to try another one?"

I grab my third card, swiping it with confidence this time, giving off the air that everything is fine.

The screen beeps again.

Declined.

"Maybe your system is down?" My question goes unanswered.

Riffling through my wallet, I discover I don't have enough cash on hand to cover this. I start mentally tallying what I can put back—anything to shrink the total and get out of here—but it's no use. The cashier's already giving me a look.

"I'll just . . . I'll come back." I gather my personal belongings—everything except my pride—and walk out of the store empty-handed. Once I hit the parking lot, I dig my phone out of my purse and open the banking app.

My first attempt to log in fails.

A stark wave of realization hits me. My hands tremble as I try again, typing the password slowly, deliberately. But the screen flashes red.

Incorrect password: one attempt remaining.

I know exactly what's happening.

Dialing Will, I grip the steering wheel with both hands. It rings once, twice, five times—before I get his voice mail.

"Will, call me back." My voice comes out clipped. I hang up and try again, but it goes straight to voice mail this time.

He's doing this on purpose.

This is his way of making sure I don't leave.

No money equals no chance to escape.

The realization hits hard and fast, stealing the breath from my lungs. For a stay-at-home mom, money is freedom. Money is autonomy. And he wasted no time taking both from me.

I grip the phone tighter, staring at the black screen, willing it to ring, for him to answer and explain.

But I already know the truth.

The account changes, the unanswered calls—it's all intentional. Last night wasn't just about his confession. It was about control. And now, without money, without access to anything, I'm trapped—exactly where he wants me.

I swallow hard, trying to tamp down the rising unease flooding through every last fiber of my being. But it claws at my throat, relentless and unforgiving.

For the first time in a long time, I'm feeling truly caged—and Will has the key.

It's taking me back to a place I thought I'd never visit again, a mental and physical prison where I'm dependent on a selfish monster who sees nothing wrong with abusing their power at my expense.

Steadying my breath, I switch the radio on and crank the volume, anything to drown out the sound of my own thoughts, which are all but demanding I do the unspeakable. But I refuse. I'm not Lucinda. I'm not Will. I'm not a murderer—because I choose not to be.

But right now, I could kill this man.

52

The smell of fish sticks fills the kitchen, a far cry from the chicken cordon bleu I'd planned to make. The kids sit at the table, kicking their legs under their chairs, too distracted by the TV in the next room to notice the subpar dinner. I set their plates down with peas scooped on the side, watching the butter slide off the vegetables and settle into a yellow pool.

Will sits at the head of the table, watching me flit around like a diner waitress. "Fish sticks, huh?"

"Change of plans," I say lightly, finally sitting down with my own plate. I spread my cloth napkin over my lap. "Dig in, everyone."

Jackson dips his fish stick into ketchup, oblivious to the tension simmering between his parents.

We eat in relative silence, broken only by the kids' chatter. Will pretends not to notice the tightness in my smile or the forced calm in my voice. When the kids finish, I usher them upstairs for their baths and help them into bed, brushing away stray giggles and good night kisses. Will reads them a short story, tucking them in with ease, as if nothing is out of the ordinary.

Tonight, more than any other night in recent months, I'd give anything for it to be just another ordinary evening.

I busy myself with laundry to avoid being alone with Will for as long as I can. By the time I'm finished, I find him in our bed grading papers, the bedside lamp casting a warm glow over his tranquil face.

How he can murder someone he hardly knows, blackmail his wife, then grade papers in their bed like it's any other night is nothing short of unsettling.

These are things people like me could do without batting an eye . . . but not someone like Will. I can numb myself to anything. Will cries at Disney movies, never passes a donation box without slipping a twenty-dollar bill inside, and volunteers at soup kitchens at Christmastime.

I hate that my children are sleeping under the same roof as someone capable of that. I hate that I'm sleeping next to him, too—but it's all part of the plan. He has to think I'm pliable, submissive, on board with this. If he thinks he's smarter than me—which he so clearly does, it's only a matter of time before he makes another dumb mistake. Until then . . . this is how it has to be.

I linger in the doorway of our bedroom, watching him. The red pen in his hand. The even rise and fall of his chest. He could be any loving husband winding down for the night—except I know better.

I cross the room and perch on the edge of the bed, gathering a breath in my lungs. "My cards got declined at the store today."

I keep my tone neutral, as if I'm simply remarking about a petty inconvenience and not pointing fingers and picking a fight.

Will doesn't look up from his paper. "Oh. Forgot to tell you. We're in the process of switching to a local bank. And I'm transferring your credit cards to ones with a lower rate. Your new cards should arrive soon."

I almost ask why he'd do that without talking to me, but I bite my tongue. I need to remain pliable, blindly obedient.

"Our old bank was based in San Diego," he says as if he senses my unasked question. He flips a page as if we're discussing the weather. "It's a logistics thing. I'd been planning to do it since we moved, just hadn't had time."

I gather a slow breath. "Is it though? The timing is . . . curious."

"It is." He moves his stack of papers to the nightstand with deliberate calm. Then he turns to me, his face unreadable minus the faintest hint of something—resolve. "But also, I have to know that I can trust you, that you're not going to take the kids and leave."

"How am I supposed to gas up the car? Buy groceries? Get things the kids need?"

He leans forward slightly. "I'll gas up your car for you. And I'll give you cash when you need it. This is just temporary. We'll get through it."

Temporary.

The word drips with condescension.

I bite the inside of my cheek to keep from saying what I truly want to say.

He shifts closer, his mood softening as he reaches for my hand. "You know I love you, right? I'm doing this because I love you."

I don't pull away, though everything inside me screams to.

"I know you better than anyone, which is why I know your instinct is to run when things get hard." His gaze bores into me. "I'm not going to let you run, Camille. I love you too much. I'm protecting you from yourself."

His thumb brushes over my knuckles. It only makes my fist clench tighter.

"You have to trust that I have our best interests at heart. Going against me would be reckless and selfish." His eyes soften, as if he's soothing a frightened child. "And you're not those things. You're a good wife, a good mother. Think of the kids. They need us. They need us together."

He leans in, grazing his lips against mine—an intimate gesture that now curdles in my chest like spoiled milk. Again, I force myself to kiss him back.

"You're right," I tell him. "I'll follow your lead on this."

He thinks he's in control.

He thinks he's won.

But he has no idea who he's kissing.

53

I sit on the couch with my laptop balanced on my knees, the screen glowing in the dim light. My heart races as I fill out the online application, typing carefully—name, address, Social Security Number. It's a shot in the dark, but I have to try. If I can get approved for a credit card, I'll at least have something . . . a way to escape with the kids when the time is right.

I click submit and hold my breath.

The answer comes almost immediately, flashing on the screen like a slap across the face.

DENIED: SSN frozen due to suspected fraud. Please contact customer service. Estimated wait time: 72 hours for resolution.

Seventy-two hours. I slam the laptop shut, pressing the heels of my hands against my eyes.

He's not just playing a game—he's playing to win. And I've made the grave mistake of underestimating him.

I pull myself together and grab my purse. I can't sit here waiting for emails or phone calls. I need access to money.

Now.

At the bank, the smell of stale coffee and disinfectant fills the air. The teller smiles politely as I fumble with my wallet, trying to maintain some semblance of normalcy. The weight of everyone's gazes presses down on me.

I glance down at my wallet, searching for my driver's license—and stop cold.

It's gone.

My heart thunders in my chest. I flip through every compartment, every pocket, tearing through the seams of leather. It's not here.

I'm paralyzed in place, my hands trembling as angry adrenaline courses through me. I can't open a new account without ID. I can't do *anything* without my license.

Will must've taken it.

I utter a quick apology to the teller and rush out of the bank, my pulse pounding in my ears. Across the way, a payday loan shop catches my eye—its neon sign buzzing faintly, promising fast cash with no questions asked.

But I don't have a paycheck. No income. No proof of anything.

The fluorescent lights hum, beckoning me, mocking me.

I turn away, swallowing the lump in my throat.

I drive in silence, heading nowhere in particular, the road stretching endlessly ahead. My mind whirls, calculating every possible option.

Several stoplights later, I pass a pawn shop and for a moment, I consider it. I could pawn something—anything—to buy myself some time. But what do I have of value?

I glance down at my hand, at the wedding ring glinting in the sunlight. It would fetch a decent amount, but if I sold it, Will would notice instantly. He's been watching me too closely, keeping tabs on every move I make. If my diamond ring went missing, he'd have questions and I'd have no way to get it back.

I can't risk setting off any alarms, not yet.

My grip tightens on the steering wheel as hopelessness creeps in. My options are dwindling. The walls are closing in, all but threatening to consume me.

I've not been this powerless since I was a child, living under Lucinda's roof.

There has to be another way.

I just have to find it.

54

The house is quiet except for the low hum of the refrigerator. The kids are fast asleep upstairs, their steady breathing the only reminder that there's still some normalcy left in this place. I sit cross-legged on the couch, phone in hand, swiping through my apps out of sheer habit.

And that's when I notice it—the Wi-Fi is off.

I tap the screen a few more times, hoping it's just a glitch, but the little icon in the corner stays stubbornly gray. I try reconnecting, but the password doesn't work.

My stomach tightens. I set my phone aside and grab my laptop, but it's the same story. Wi-Fi network locked. Password changed.

Anger bubbles under my skin, but it turns cold when I glance back at my phone and notice something else—a little arrow along the top of the screen telling me my location tracking is active.

Pulling up the settings, I attempt to turn location tracking off, only to get a message telling me that setting is locked under parental controls. I swipe again, tapping deeper into the restrictions menu, but it's useless. Everything is locked tight, and I know without asking who did it.

I take my phone and head to the bedroom, where Will is propped against the pillows, reading a medical journal like everything is fine. He glances up when I walk in, his expression neutral—as if none of this is a big deal. If this man were a complete stranger to me, I'd assume he didn't have a care in the entire world.

While I'd love to toss the phone at him, I tamp down the urge and instead offer a casual, "Honey, did you change the Wi-Fi password?"

He doesn't look surprised. "I didn't have a choice."

"And you turned on location tracking on my phone? Under parental settings?"

He sighs, closing his periodical and placing it on the nightstand. "This is an extreme situation. It called for extreme precautions. Again, it's all temporary."

Fury is barely contained beneath my surface, but on the outside I'm as collected as ever. "Taking my ID, freezing my credit, locking me out of everything? A little overkill, don't you think? There needs to be trust going both ways if we're going to rebuild it."

He leans forward, his expression understanding but deliberate. "I get your frustration, but I can't risk having you googling things that might implicate you—or us—in anything."

His tone is measured, like he's trying to reason with a child.

It makes my skin crawl yet satisfies me at the same time because it tells me he's still underestimating me.

"And the tracking?" I ask, fluttering my lashes.

"That's for safety," he says simply, as if that explains everything. "I need to know where you are at all times, especially since the kids are always with you."

"You keep saying that." I take a slow breath, trying to keep my voice steady. "But how am I supposed to feel safe when you're threatening to pin Sozi's murder on me if I tell anyone? That doesn't make me feel safe? And when you take away my ability to buy groceries? How am I supposed to trust you? You say you have our family's best interest at heart, but it sounds to me like you're only serving your own."

He studies me for a long moment, his face unreadable.

I still don't know what he did with her body or how he cleaned it up so meticulously without me knowing he was even there—but the less I know, the better. Knowing anything would make me an accomplice after the fact.

"I didn't say I *would* pin it on you," he says. "I said I've taken precautions to protect our family. There's a difference."

I shake my head, disbelief washing over me. I'm not mincing words with him. I know exactly what he said and exactly what he meant.

"How exactly do you plan on pinning it on me?" I ask. "I was with the kids the entire time."

Will leans back against the pillows, his expression cool.

"I've got it figured out," he says. "I hope you understand that I can't reveal all my cards."

His words are laced with arrogance. I search his face, trying to decide if he's bluffing. But the thing about Will is, I wouldn't know what bluffing looks like on him. He's never had to bluff before. He's always been a straight shooter—or so I mistakenly believed.

He's thought this through, every step. I can't tell if he's waiting for me to slip, or if he's already set the trap and is just watching to see when I'll step into it.

Instead, I pull the mask over my face, the one I've worn for years. I smile—small, careful, measured. "I understand. I'd do the same thing in your shoes."

And it's true.

I would.

I'd do it ten times worse, though.

He's a rookie.

His posture turns relaxed, like a man who's won some small victory.

"Good." He reaches, pulling me close. "You know I love you, right? And I'm doing this for us."

I do know that—Will reminds me every chance he gets.

"We're lucky to have you," I practically coo into his ear as I wrap my arms around him tight. He all but melts against me. "And I can't wait until we right this ship."

55

I leave my phone on the kitchen counter, tucked beneath a stack of unopened mail. Will tracks my every move now, and I need just one day—*one day*—without his watchful eye.

The consignment shops that give cash on the spot are few and far between, scattered across town, hole-in-the-wall places crammed with clothes and shoes that smell faintly of mothballs, perfume, and time. I wander through each one, handing over whatever I can: Georgie's ballet flats from last year, a few higher-end boutique dresses she's already outgrown, Jackson's like-new Nike sneakers, and some of my own upscale pieces—things I haven't worn since San Diego.

They won't be missed. Will never notices what we wear. He doesn't do laundry; he doesn't know the inventory of our closets.

At every shop, I act cordial and friendly, attempting to look natural, but my heart pounds with every item they toss in the "buy" pile. I watch the numbers climb on the register in each store, only for the final payout to fall short of what I need.

When the sun dips low on the horizon, I'm left with a handful of cash: $287. It's wrinkled and pitiful in my wallet, but it's enough for two tanks of gas, some gas station meals, maybe a dingy motel for a couple of nights.

But I still have no plan. No one to run to.

Without real money, I wouldn't be able to keep us hidden for long. I could drive somewhere, sure, but Will would find us. Eventually.

I swallow the knot forming in my throat, push my grave concerns down for now, and pick up the kids from school. They chatter happily in the back seat, oblivious to the storm cloud gathering inside me.

When we pull into the driveway, I find Will standing in front of the house, talking to Mara and Oscar.

A week ago, my vision would've blurred red at this sight.

Now? I'm just annoyed. What's his angle? What's he trying to accomplish? Is he arrogant . . . or just plain stupid?

After what he did, he shouldn't be talking to anyone—especially loose cannons like the Morenos. Besides, Will and I still have yet to discuss the dating app thing. Strangely, it's as if he's been going out of his way to avoid the conversation altogether, and with everything going on, I'm not about to open another can of worms.

I park and tell the kids to head inside, giving them an absent smile that doesn't reach my eyes. Strolling over, I maintain a dignified posture.

"Camille, have you heard from Sozi lately?" Mara asks.

My breath hitches, but I force a neutral expression. "No, why?"

Mara's brows knit. "She's got packages piling up at her door. I've never seen that happen, not in all the years we've lived here."

Oscar shifts uncomfortably, glancing toward the house. "Maybe she's just out of town."

I exchange a quick look with Will, who remains composed—too composed. His gaze meets mine with a quiet warning not to say anything.

"I haven't heard from her," I say. "Not for a few days, now that you mention it."

Mara peers toward Sozi's house again, her mouth twisting at one side.

"It's weird," she muses, more to herself than to us.

Oscar nudges her. "Let's just take the packages inside. Put them in her garage like we did last time she went out of town. Assuming the code hasn't changed."

If the Morenos see Sozi's car in the garage, they'll know she's not out of town. They'll know Sozi hasn't gone anywhere. And if Mara tells any other neighbors on Saguaro Circle about those packages and the police get involved—the text messages between Sozi and me will be the first thing they uncover.

I'll be their first suspect.

My jaw clenches so tight it sends a shock of pain up the side of my head.

The Morenos aren't going to sit idly by. When they realize Sozi hasn't returned for days, weeks, or months . . . they're going to say something.

It's only a matter of time before this plays out—in the worst way.

I only wish I knew how much time I had.

Later that night, after the kids are in bed, I find Will at the kitchen table, scrolling through something on his laptop. I take the chair across from him, my hands folded in my lap, shoulders straight and head held high.

"We need to talk about the cameras," I say.

Will's eyes lift slowly from his screen, unreadable. "What about them?"

"If ours weren't working, maybe the Morenos' or Sozi's cameras caught something—like her coming over and not leaving."

Will's expression doesn't change, but something flickers in his eyes—something dark. "The Morenos' cameras don't reach our driveway. Oscar mentioned that back when Mara went missing."

I bite my lip. "Sozi's?"

He closes the laptop with a soft click, as if sealing the conversation. "I disabled them."

A cold knot tightens in my throat. "How?"

Will leans back in his chair, folding his arms. "I used her fingerprint to unlock her security app, then I deleted the videos from that day— and the ones before it—then I disabled the camera altogether."

The room suddenly feels smaller, more suffocating than ever.

"So there's no proof of her coming here?" I ask. "No footage?"

He shakes his head slowly, his gaze never leaving mine. "None."

The weight of what he's just said settles over me, cold and heavy. He's thought of everything. Every loose thread tied off. Every piece of evidence wiped away.

There's a chance *I've* underestimated *him.*

"Camille, can I say something?" His words are as cold and haunting as the look in his eyes. "You've been so understanding with everything, and I just wanted to thank you for that. I know it hasn't been easy. And it's not going to be easy. But knowing we're on the same page, that you trust my decisions . . ."

I swallow as he rambles on, nodding and smiling and giving him as much nonverbal reassurance as I can, but inside, my mind is racing, frantically searching for a way out of this prison he's built. Because if I don't find a way soon, there won't be one.

56

The fluorescent lights in the donation center buzz overhead, making my head throb as I sit on the vinyl recliner, trying not to look at the needle in my arm. The tube snakes from the crook of my elbow, carrying my blood to the machine, where it spins away the plasma before pumping what's left back into me.

The technician hums quietly, not noticing how my vein bulges painfully around the needle. It's the third attempt today. My veins are stubborn, the kind that roll out of reach or collapse under pressure. I shouldn't be doing this, but I don't have a choice.

When it's finally over, my arm feels heavy and numb. I pocket the crumpled bills—barely enough to cover a couple of tanks of gas—and walk out into the blinding sunlight, wondering how the hell I'm going to keep this up.

This isn't sustainable. Not with these veins. Not with the bruising that's already starting to spread beneath the bandage. Will is going to notice. Maybe not this time because I'll take precautions, but I can't hide something like this for long.

◆ ◆ ◆

At dinner, I sit across from Will, discreetly rubbing my arm under the table. The ache in my vein throbs with each beat of my heart, radiating through my elbow and down to my wrist. I adjust the sleeve of my sweater to make sure it covers the forming bruise.

The kids yammer between bites of spaghetti, oblivious as always. Will studies me, as if waiting for the right moment to say something. He never just blurts things out anymore—he's too calculated for that.

Once the kids scamper off to the living room, meals half finished, Will leans back in his chair and folds his arms. "Mara and Oscar are starting to ask a lot of questions."

I lift my chin high, appearing unworried. "What kind of questions?"

"Well, they're presenting theories, mostly, asking me what I think." He seems unbothered except for the tension in his jaw. "I tried to shut them down, but they're persistent. They also think they should take care of Sozi's packages until she gets back. I told them you'd handle it."

I suppress the urge to snap at him. Of course I'll be the one stuck with that. If I do get implicated in this, that'll only make me look guiltier in retrospect.

"There's more," he says, watching my reaction. "I'm going to send a few texts between your phone and Sozi's tomorrow—make it look like she's alive, still in touch."

"Won't the location be obvious?"

He shakes his head. "I won't do it at work. I'll do it from somewhere generic—the grocery store, a gas station. Places without any connection to us."

"With all due respect, you're not a criminal mastermind, Will. You're a doctor. Don't get cocky about this."

He reaches across the table and takes my hand, giving it a gentle squeeze that tightens at the very end.

"You have to trust me," he says.

I force a smile, but inside, the word "trust" feels like ash on my tongue.

I'll never be able to trust him again.

◆ ◆ ◆

Later that night, I rest on the edge of the bed, going over the numbers in my head. I have to play this carefully if I want to stay afloat.

"Jackson needs new soccer cleats," I tell him, keeping my voice casual. "They're a hundred dollars. And Georgie's ballet lessons for the month are due tomorrow. Those are two fifty."

Will pulls his wallet from the nightstand without hesitation, thumbing through twenties and fifties. He hands me the exact amount, his eyes locking with mine. "Please give me the receipts when you're done."

I bite the inside of my cheek and nod. "I also need to pick up groceries. Those are usually a couple hundred, sometimes more."

"Order them on the app," he says. "Use my card to pay. You can hot spot my phone."

I give a small, tight-lipped smile.

The next morning, I sit at the kitchen table, scrolling through the grocery store's app on my phone. I load the cart with the basics—bread, milk, snacks for the kids. Then I throw in a few high-ticket items: a couple of moderately priced skincare items, a tablet, a new air fryer. Nothing too outrageous. I need to stay under the radar.

At checkout, I add a couple of Visa gift cards—balances just enough to avoid suspicion. Once the groceries are delivered, I'll head straight to the store and return the high-dollar items for cash or store credit. I'll pocket whatever I can, siphoning off small amounts week by week until I have enough.

It's a slow, careful game. But I'll play it for as long as I have to.

That evening, as we lie in bed, the mood is quietly oppressive, filled with unspoken tension—at least for me. Will flips through his medical journal, his mind already elsewhere, as if nothing about this situation fazes him.

"How long is this going to last?" I break the silence.

"As long as necessary." He folds the periodical closed and turns to me with raised brows. "I think we're doing just fine, though, don't you? You have everything you need. The kids do, too. Like I said, it's only temporary for you."

If only he knew just how temporary this is going to be for him . . .

57

I'm cross-legged on the bedroom floor, cash spread out in neat stacks in front of me. Each bill is a tiny victory, scraped together from returns, consignment sales, and the gift card hustle I've been running all month. I've managed to amass just under $2,000.

It's not nearly enough—not for a clean break. Not to keep the kids fed, sheltered, and hidden for long. But it's something. A small lifeline.

The problem isn't just leaving—it's staying gone. Any electronic purchase or movement will leave a trail Will could follow in an instant. He has eyes everywhere, systems in place. I know him too well to think otherwise. He'd track me the second I stepped out of his control.

I could request the Social Security Card for Gabrielle Nichols—my legal name—but it'll take time. And once the card arrives, I'll have to monitor the mailbox like a hawk to make sure he doesn't intercept it.

If Will gets that card before I do? Game over.

I rub my temple, feeling the weight of the situation press down on me like a thousand bricks. Every move has to be precise. If I slip up even once, he'll tighten his grip. And if he catches wind that I'm planning to run, there'll be no escape.

Through the bedroom window, I can hear laughter floating up from the backyard. I stand and peek through the curtains. Will's in the pool playing with the kids. Georgie shrieks with delight as he tosses her into the air, water splashing everywhere as she lands with a giggle. Jackson clings to his back, pretending to wrestle him.

They look so happy.

So normal.

But they have no idea.

No idea that the man in the pool with them is a murderer, no idea that he's diabolically controlling every part of my life. They're none the wiser that the father they adore is no better than the one person I've spent my life running from.

Will is a stranger to us all.

But worse than that, he's also a self-centered monster, capable of hurting people, of taking innocent lives. Sozi was far from perfect, but she didn't deserve to die so that Will could have the life he wanted.

It pains me to take this from them, but I don't have a choice.

I refuse to let them be raised by a variant of Jacqueline Prescott. I didn't go through what I went through and build from scratch a life that looks like this . . . only to have children who grow up learning the fine art of being unsuspectingly diabolical.

Jacqueline and Lucinda are two sides of the same coin.

But Will? He *is* the coin.

I press my forehead to the cool glass, watching the scene outside with clenched fists. Will splashing, laughing, playing the part of the perfect father.

I step back from the window, a cold determination settling over me like armor.

58

The house is silent, the kind of stillness that only comes in the dead of night. I slip quietly out of bed, every muscle tensed, listening for any sign of Will stirring. He doesn't. His steady breathing fills the room, and I tiptoe toward the door, the prepaid phone I purchased earlier today clutched in my hand.

In the hallway, I crouch in a dark corner. It's the safest place—close enough to hear if Will wakes, far enough from the bedroom to avoid his scrutiny. I unlock the phone, open a private browser just in case, and start typing.

"Lucinda Dawn Nichols."

I've avoided this search for years, terrified of what I might find. But now? I need to know.

Results flood the screen, but they're mostly old, scattered reports from the past. She's a ghost. A remnant of the life I left behind.

Then I find something new—Lucinda Dawn McClindon. Exact same birthdate. Residing in Illinois.

It has to be her.

I use one of the prepaid Visa cards to run a background check, my hands trembling as I input the payment information. A few minutes later, the results load.

Lucinda is living in Schaumburg, Illinois, in a sprawling $3 million brick colonial with a circle drive, guest quarters above a four-car garage, and an in-ground pool. It's the kind of neighborhood with meticulously trimmed hedges, luxury SUVs in the driveway, and homeowners' association rules about lawn decor.

According to this, she's married to a man named Robert McClindon, a prominent figure in the Chicago financial industry.

A quick social media search tells me they do, in fact, have a daughter. For once, she wasn't lying.

The girl has Lucinda's sharp cheekbones and delicate nose—but the coffee-brown eyes with the flare of hazel in the middle . . .

They're mine.

She looks to be roughly thirteen, which means Lucinda had her not long after I left.

I study the curated images of a half sister I never knew existed. The resemblance is undeniable.

Does she do to this child what she did to me?

Is their brick McMansion another facade for a house of horrors?

The girl looks happy in the photos—much happier than I ever did at that age.

And Lucinda's life looks perfect—curated to the point of obsession. Social media photos show staged family dinners, tropical cruises, the daughter's dance recitals, and charity events attended in gowns worth more than I've ever had in my savings account.

She's built an existence that looks more polished and untouchable than my own.

It dawns on me that perhaps Lucinda has never come looking for me. She's set for life—married to a man with money, living in a mansion, raising his child. She has everything she's ever wanted, and with a daughter to secure her financial future, she doesn't need me anymore. She has too much to lose by doing anything reckless, by acting on an age-old vendetta.

The idea that she might have never even looked for me stings in a way I wasn't prepared for. I swallow the lump forming in my throat and push that thought aside. It doesn't matter. What matters is that she's there. Hiding in plain sight. It somehow makes her less . . . daunting . . . to think about.

She has too much to lose by doing anything crazy.

It's been weeks since she's sent a letter.

The last one contained her phone number—maybe that was her final olive branch? Her last attempt before whatever game she was playing started to bore her?

I stare at the screen, contemplating something unthinkable— reaching out to her for help.

The thought alone makes my stomach burn with bile. I'd never trust her alone with Jack or Georgie. *Never.* Lucinda might look domesticated now, but I know better. She's the same woman who made my life a living hell. Those designer clothes and expensive zip code don't make her any less of a monster.

But she has what I need—money. And most importantly, it would be the absolute last place on earth Will would ever think to look for us.

It's a twisted safety net only Lucinda could offer—if I could even talk her into it.

Hell, if I could talk *myself* into it . . .

I close my eyes and take a breath, hating myself for so much as considering it.

But what other options do I have?

I screenshot photos of her information—Lucinda's new name, her address, the smiling family photo of her perfect little life—and save it to a hidden photo file on my burner phone. Then I close the app and slip the phone into my pocket, my heart pounding as I tiptoe back to bed. I slide under the sheets, careful not to disturb Will. He rustles but doesn't wake.

I imagine the day he comes home to an empty house.

59

Today is the day.

I finish getting ready and return to the kitchen where my children are finishing breakfast.

"Guess what, guys? We're having a special mommy day. No school today. Just us." My smile is bright yet my eyes are empty, a marquee without a show.

Jackson's eyes light. The kid lives for surprises.

Georgiana, more skeptical and becoming more aware by the day, tilts her head. "What about Daddy?"

"Daddy's working late tonight. It'll just be our little adventure. How does that sound?" I lean down and kiss her forehead, smoothing her wild locks. She shrugs but doesn't argue as she shovels another spoonful of cereal into her mouth.

After breakfast, I pack snacks and waters into Georgiana's pink backpack and grab Jackson's favorite toy train. Essentials. Nothing to indicate we're not coming back. My hands tremble as I toss Lucinda's letters into a trash bag, the words inked in venom, their weight unbearable. As soon as we're on the road, I plan to toss them out the window on some lonely stretch of highway—no cameras, no witnesses.

Will can't know about those letters. Ever.

We load up as soon as the kids are done eating.

By the time I hit the first ATM, my pulse is racing. While Will showered this morning, I slipped his credit cards from his wallet and prayed to a god I've never believed in that he wouldn't notice.

Today that god finally came through for me.

The camera above the keypad watches me like a hawk, but I've planned for this. Baseball cap, sunglasses, and hair tucked under a hoodie makes it look like I'm running—which is intentional. If and when Will gets these cash advance notifications and if and when the police pull the footage, they'll think I'm dressed like I'm in hiding. That's what they'll be looking for. Not someone hiding in plain sight.

First card, $500.

Second card, another $500.

I hit four more machines before I've maxed out his cash advance limit. Five thousand dollars. Added to the two thousand I've been squirreling away, it's enough to get us out.

Not far. But out.

The kids are blissfully unaware, playing with their tablets in the back seat as I pull into a gas station parking lot outside of East Mesa, where a rusted-out four-door 2002 Chevy Cavalier waits. The man selling it looks like he's never met a toothbrush he liked.

"Runs great. Belonged to my grandma before she died." The faint scent of stale cigarettes clings to his words as he marinates us both in the stench of adult male body odor.

The Facebook Marketplace ad said it had "fifty-six thousand well-maintained" miles. Low for its age. And I've done my homework. This model's reliable enough.

"I'll throw in a couple extra gallons of gas for ya." He grins, revealing teeth that favor a picket fence after a hurricane.

I hand over the seventeen hundred in cash we agreed on over the phone yesterday afternoon, and he passes me one set of keys.

I never thought freedom would smell like nicotine, but alas, it does.

I transfer the kids into the Cavalier while they pepper me with questions.

"Why are we taking this car, Mommy?" Jackson asks.

Georgiana wrinkles her nose. "Why does it stink in here?"

"Because it's special," I say. "Like today."

My daughter doesn't buy it, but she doesn't push. Will's first text pings my phone as I'm buckling Jackson's seat belt. I knew it wouldn't take long.

WILL: Where are you?

A second follows almost immediately: Call me. Now.

I slide into the driver's seat and start the engine. It coughs to life, rattling like a smoker's last breath.

Another text lights up the screen: Don't do this, Camille.

By the time I hit the interstate, the texts have turned venomous. You're not going to get away with this. You're making a HUGE mistake. Come back NOW.

I glance at the phone, the lifeline tethering me to the life I'm severing. Then I roll down the window and toss it out, watching it shatter apart on the asphalt in the rearview mirror.

The kids don't notice. Jackson is singing to himself. Georgiana's staring out her window, lost in her own world. My chest tightens as I death-grip the steering wheel.

I contemplate the events of the last two months, fitting them all into context so I can understand how I got here.

It doesn't take long for me to boil it down to one thing.

Jealousy.

It turns out, when you have something other people want . . . a thriving, satisfying marriage to a doctor, a comfortable suburban life, a happy family, and a loving home . . . some of those people will stop at nothing to try and take it from you.

Sozi desperately wanted something that felt the way my life looked, and it cost her her life. If Mara hadn't spent so much energy envying my marriage, she might have saved herself the humiliation of that cringeworthy disappearing stunt.

And Will's raging jealousy over the assumption that I was going to leave him for Oscar brought out the worst in him. In the end, he forever lost the very thing he was so fraught to keep.

Sometimes I wonder if Lucinda was jealous of me. I was a happy child. At least at first. I was innocent. Untainted by the ugliness of the real world—until she made it her personal mission to steal the light from my eyes, to make me as miserable as she was.

My children will *never* know that feeling.

I dream up the kind of life I want for them, the life I'll stop at nothing to give them. But in order to make that happen, I have to get them far away from this one—away from the man who wants to take me out of the picture.

For now, there's only one place I can go to ensure Will can never find us—so I drive east.

60

I'm parked at a gas station somewhere in East Texas, gripping my cheap prepaid phone so hard it might snap in two. The screen is dim in the evening sun, but Lucinda's number is queued up, glowing like a curse. My palms are damp, and the knot in my throat twists tighter with each second that passes.

In the rearview, I watch my children sleep, their little faces bathed in peace and naivety—just the way I intend to keep it.

My thumb hovers over the call button, and I take a deep breath.

Then I tap the button before I can talk myself out of it.

The phone rings once.

Twice.

Three times.

Each ring sends my heart thundering harder, threatening to crack my ribs. Sweat beads along my hairline. My hand shakes. Bile burns my throat. It's been a while since I've had a visceral reaction this intense.

The line goes quiet mid-ring.

A woman's voice—smooth and sharp, exactly how I remember—fills the line. "Hello?"

My throat tightens. I have to force the words out, my birth name. "It's Gabrielle."

The silence that follows stretches like a knife's edge, cutting into me. I expect something cruel, sarcastic—maybe a click as she hangs up without another word.

"Gabrielle?" My name is whisper soft on her voice as she stretches each syllable.

There's something unsettling in the way she says it—not quite disbelief but something close.

Then she's silent again, and I wonder if this is where she'll deny knowing me. If she'll play dumb, pretend she doesn't recognize the name I've carried with me like a scar for years.

The seconds tick by, each one more weighted than the last. And then, finally, she speaks again.

"I didn't think you'd call," she says, a hint of a smile in her tone. "But I can't tell you how happy I am that you did."

Her words land like they're stitched together from pieces of someone else's voice. There's what sounds like genuine warmth, sincerity. If I didn't know her better, I'd believe it, too.

It's an act. It always is with her.

But I'm in a desperate place. I can't afford to care if she means it or not. My life—my children's lives—depend on this.

"Do you have time to talk?" she asks.

"Not really," I say, my voice tight. "I'm calling because . . ."

My throat is dry, my lips refusing to form the words they so desperately need to.

On the other end of the line, Lucinda doesn't press me. She doesn't ask where I've been or why I left. She's waiting. Waiting for me to speak, to hand over the power. The less one person talks, the more likely it is the other person will volunteer information—a "trick" she taught me a lifetime ago.

I close my eyes for a second, forcing down the nausea rising in my throat. I never thought it would come to this. Never thought I'd be the one reaching out to her for anything, let alone something as grave as this.

"I'm calling because," I try again, "I need your help with something."

But the last thing I'll ever do—the thing I can't let happen, no matter what—is leave my children to be raised by someone like Will, another manipulative monster, just like the one on the other end of this phone.

Just like the one who raised him.

I don't want to do this, but I don't have a choice if I want to keep my children safe.

Will is a hornet whose nest has just been kicked. He's fired up. Furious. Determined. Reactive. Lucinda has had over a decade to calm down since our altercation. Of the two monsters, she's the sounder of the two right now—something I never imagined would happen in this lifetime.

I grip the steering wheel with my free hand, steadying myself as the fluorescent lights of the gas station grow blurry and out of focus. I don't know where this conversation will lead, but one thing is clear: there's nothing I wouldn't do if it means keeping my children safe.

Even if it means trusting the one woman I know I shouldn't: the devil herself.

My grip tightens on the wheel until my knuckles pierce white through my skin. I've got nowhere else to go and she has money and a large house and enough incentive not to do anything reckless.

Lucinda, for better or worse, is my best bet until I can get on my feet and figure out the next move.

"What is it, Gabrielle?" she asks, her voice almost singsong. She's thrilled that I'm asking for her help. The desperation feeds her soul. I can *feel* it. "What's going on?"

"It's a long story." Glancing in the rearview, I check on my sleeping children in the back seat, two innocent babies blissfully unaware of the dark tide I'm steering us into. "Can I tell you in person?"

My only job in this world is to keep my children safe, to protect them from harm. And that's what I'll continue to do. If Lucinda takes us in, I won't let them out of my sight for a minute. There won't be a single morsel of food that passes from Lucinda's hands to their lips. I'll supervise each and every conversation.

I'll make this work.

I have to.

I pull onto the highway, my headlights carving into the night shadows, each mile heavier than the one before. It's almost as if the road itself is begging me to slow down, to turn around, to stop.

But I don't.

Because the only way out of this storm is through it.

Epilogue

WILL

I step into the house after work, and the instant silence strikes me like a cold, hard slap despite the fact that I knew I'd be coming home to this. Still, nothing could've prepared me for the deafening lack of laughter, cartoons, and little feet pattering across the floor. Nothing but a void and Camille's meticulous order.

The kids' shoes aren't by the door. Georgiana's favorite pink backpack—the one she drags everywhere—is absent. Jackson's blue train, the one he takes everywhere lately, is nowhere to be found. Reality clicks into place faster than I'd like to admit, faster than I want to accept.

My phone is already in my hand. Her number. Dialed. Straight to voice mail. A muscle in my jaw tightens, but I keep my cool. I dial again, just to make sure. Nothing.

She hasn't replied to any of my texts from earlier, so I don't expect her to answer my calls, but it doesn't stop me from trying.

My lips twitch into something that's not quite a smile. I'd always had my suspicions about Camille, suspecting there was more to her than met the eye. No one is *that* perfect. But my uncertainties weren't confirmed until my mother let the cat out of the bag last year with Camille's diagnosis.

Unbeknownst to my wife, we're two sides of the same coin in many ways. Learning about her diagnosis only helped me understand her better so I could keep a tighter leash on her and maintain the control I spent our entire marriage letting her think she had.

But leaving me? Taking the kids? That wasn't part of the game.

My hand clenches into a fist so tight it sends a shock of pain up my forearm. Eyeing the nearest wall, I fight the urge to punch it.

I want to.

But I don't.

Because there's power in control, and power is what I have in spades.

I call my wife again. Voice mail. A third time. Voice mail. My calm fractures. My thumb hovers, then swipes over another name in my contacts.

Sozi.

She answers on the second ring, her voice soft but wary. "Will?"

"She's gone," I say, my voice even, deliberate.

There's a pause, and I know she's calculating. Always thinking, always trying to anticipate me. She couldn't if she tried. She's not as intelligent, not nearly as cunning. That's why I picked her as my affair partner. We met at a hotel bar years ago, when I was in Boston for a medical conference and she was in town visiting family for a reunion. She was distractingly gorgeous—which drew my eye. And after buying her a drink and talking to her, it didn't take long for me to ascertain she was perfect for me . . . for what I wanted, for what I needed.

She was weak. Unsure of herself. Mentally unstable enough to not cause problems but enough that she'd be easy to control. She lapped up my attention like a relapsing addict, and by the end of the night, when I took her back to my hotel room, she was putty in my hands.

The woman didn't bat a lash when I told her I needed her to fake her death in my garage so I could get a better handle on Camille. She even did it all herself, followed my instructions to the letter. I didn't have to leave work.

"What do you mean, *gone*?" Sozi asks.

"Exactly what I said. Camille left. Took the kids." I pause, letting the words hang. "I just got home and the house is empty. She's not answering her phone. The kids' things are gone."

"I told you she was unstable," Sozi says after a moment, her tone edging toward smug. She's been trying to convince me to leave my wife for a couple of years now. It was never going to happen, but letting Sozi think there's a chance keeps her compliant and loyal. "You didn't want to hear it."

"Unstable?" I let out a soft laugh. "Sozi, if Camille is unstable, what does that make you?"

I shouldn't have said that. My emotions are running too high for my own good. "Unstable" is a sharp word to use on people who don't realize they're unstable. It cuts them like a surgical blade. The last time I said that to Sozi, I was attempting to demonstrate how fucked up it was that she was befriending my wife—and the whole wine bottle and note from "M" was unnecessary. I told her she was above that despite knowing damn well she wasn't. But I had to get her under control. She was getting carried away and that was my fault. I knew moving next door to her was going to be risky, but it was the challenge of it that excited me. Except in doing so, I got Sozi's hopes up a little too high. It emboldened her in ways it shouldn't have.

There's a sharp intake of breath on the other end of the line, and for a second, I think Sozi might hang up. But she doesn't. She never does.

"What do you want me to do?" she asks, her voice softer now, pliant. "Can I come back home?"

Sozi's death was supposed to be my masterpiece, the move that put Camille exactly where I needed her. After finding that app on her phone, I thought she was going to leave me for that sad sack of shit next door—which would've been humiliating and financially ruinous. And when she found out about my contact with my mother, that presented an entirely new set of issues. Staging Sozi's death gave me two things: a way to keep Camille silent about my mother's no-contact violation, and a lock on her loyalty.

I lean against the kitchen counter, exhaling slowly as I pinch the bridge of my nose. Tension coils at my temples, pounding in time with each heavy thump of my heart.

"She's going to regret this," I say, more to myself than to Sozi.

"What's the plan?" Sozi asks, her voice almost trembling with eagerness. It's sickening how predictable she is, how desperate for my approval. But that's what makes her useful. Minus the meddling she did when she felt threatened by Mara's flirtations—the necklace, the letter, the constant planting of seeds in Camille's mind about Mara—Sozi's come in quite handy since we moved. After nipping some things in the bud, I was able to rein in Sozi's crazy to a controllable level again, but it took a bit of finessing.

"Our plan?" I repeat, a smile curling at the corners of my lips as I emphasize the word "our." I need her to believe she's not the replaceable pawn she truly is. "Our plan is simple. I find my kids. I bring them home. And Camille learns what happens when you play games with someone who doesn't lose."

"And Camille?" Sozi ventures. "What are you going to do with her? Surely you're not going to stay married after all of this, are you?"

I don't answer. Instead, I glance at the family portrait above the fireplace. The perfect illusion. The perfect lie. My fist clenches at my side. I had it all. Loving wife. A beautiful daughter, an adorable son. A successful career. Status. Privilege. Respect. A mother who worshipped the ground I walked on.

Camille has taken *everything* from me.

I'll get it back.

All of it.

But first, I have to find her—and I will because I know my wife.

I know her better than she thinks I do.

While it won't be easy, it won't be impossible either.

Not for me.

And certainly not for a man with nothing more to lose.

Acknowledgments

For this book—and for reasons I couldn't possibly express with a single page—my gratitude runs deep.

To Jessica Tribble Wells and Charlotte Herscher—your insight, patience, and dedication to this story have been invaluable. Thank you for pushing me to make this book the best it could be.

To my incredible team at Thomas & Mercer—your support and passion for my work never cease to amaze me.

To my agent, Jill, at Marsal Lyon Literary Agency—thank you for your tireless efforts as you help guide and shape the career of my dreams.

To Maxine and Leslie, two of my favorite humans and confidantes, thank you for being my sounding boards and cheerleaders. Your unwavering encouragement keeps me grounded and your advice keeps me sane.

To the die-hard readers, librarians, and book influencers who champion my stories, thank you for your enthusiasm and for keeping the conversation going. Your support gives me life.

To my three beautiful children, thank you for eating frozen pizza for dinner more than you'd like the weeks I'm deep in the writing cave. Being your mother is my favorite (except when you're fighting). ☺

I'd be remiss if I didn't acknowledge the real-life sociopath I chanced upon after writing the first book in this series. Those whirlwind six weeks were equal parts unsettling and illuminating, but they provided me with profound insight into the mind of someone with this disorder. For that, I am oddly grateful.

Finally, a most special thank-you to Michael.

Book Club Questions

1. Camille is a diagnosed sociopath. How did her perspective influence your feelings toward her? Did you find yourself empathizing with her despite her nature? Why or why not?

2. How would you describe Camille's relationship with her husband, Will? Do you think he truly knows her, or is he part of the "perfect facade" she's constructed? How does his role as a husband and father evolve throughout the story?

3. What do you think the letters from Camille's mother reveal about her traumatic past? How do they shape Camille's actions and fears in her new life in Arizona?

4. Sozi, the new neighbor, has a dynamic personality. In what ways does Sozi's presence challenge Camille?

5. How does the volatile relationship between Oscar and Mara mirror or contrast with Camille's own marriage? What do you think Camille's interactions with them say about her ability (or inability) to feel compassion or attachment?

6. Will's mother seems to hold power over him and the family dynamic despite their estrangement. How does her nonphysical presence complicate Camille's attempts to control her carefully curated life?

7. Camille is both fiercely protective of her children and detached from traditional maternal emotions. How does this dichotomy

affect her relationship with Georgiana and Jackson? How do her actions as a mother shape the story?

8. Much of the tension in the book revolves around Camille's desire to maintain control while chaos brews around her. How do her efforts to keep control both succeed and fail? What does this say about her true vulnerabilities?

9. The title, *Circle of Strangers*, reflects the various relationships in Camille's new life. In what ways are the people in her orbit—her neighbors, family, and friends—strangers to her? How does this concept tie into the story's central mystery?

10. Given the glimpses into Camille's past and her mother's psychological manipulation, do you think Camille's sociopathy was inevitable? How does this knowledge affect your judgment of her character?

About the Author

Photo © 2024 Jill Austin

Minka Kent is the *Washington Post* and *Wall Street Journal* bestselling author of *Imaginary Strangers, After Dark, The Watcher Girl, When I Was You, The Stillwater Girls, The Thinnest Air, The Perfect Roommate, The Memory Watcher, Unmissing, The Silent Woman, Gone Again*, and *People Like Them*. Her work has been featured in *People* magazine and the *New York Post* and has been nominated for two International Thriller Awards, an Audie, and a Shirley Jackson Award. Her novel *Unmissing* was adapted for Lifetime in 2024. Minka also writes contemporary romance as *Wall Street Journal* and #1 Amazon Charts bestselling author Winter Renshaw. For more information, visit https://minkakent.com.

WELCOME TO THE NEIGHBORHOOD.
WATCH YOUR BACK.

Camille and Will Prescott have relocated from San Diego to Phoenix for a fresh start in a quiet gated community. After the traumas Camille's marriage survived, it's just the sanctuary she needs. As for her new neighbors, there's Sozi, seemingly well intentioned if not for her invasive meddling and her desperate overtures to make a friend. And Mara and Oscar, an unstable couple around whom troubling rumors swirl.

Patiently listening to Sozi's gossip and watching Mara and Oscar ever so closely has become something of a hobby for Camille. But while she obsesses about the cracks in everyone else's lives, she begins to see the cracks in her own. And when a monster from her past reaches out to reconnect, it's all Camille can do not to snap. Then one day she finds a dead body in her garage lying in a pool of blood.

Camille is about to discover what's really going on behind the closed doors of this cozy cul-de-sac. And the worst is yet to come.

ISBN 978-1662527012
US $16.99
51699
9 781662 527012

THOMAS & MERCER